GERTIE'S GREEN THUMB

Soon the Darnfields had kicked off their boots and were going barefoot in the fresh grass. It felt cool and silky beneath their feet. The grass kept growing thicker, and it spread everywhere: through the rooms on the first floor and up the stairs and all across the second floor. When Mrs. Darnfield saw how nicely the green things were growing, she decided to start an herb garden in one corner of the kitchen. (She said she had always believed in being adaptable.) She planted thyme and parsley and dill and sage. In other rooms, she planted tulip bulbs and lettuce and peas. Everything sprouted overnight and grew much faster than it would have in an ordinary garden. "You'd almost think those vegetables grew by magic," said Mrs. Darnfield.

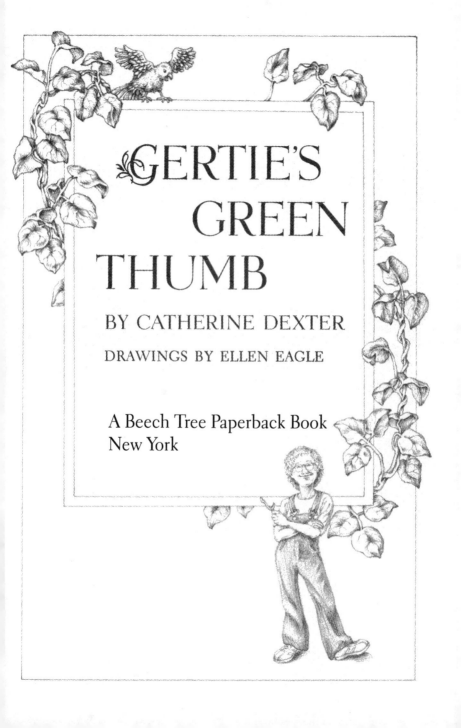

GERTIE'S GREEN THUMB

BY CATHERINE DEXTER

DRAWINGS BY ELLEN EAGLE

A Beech Tree Paperback Book
New York

LIBRARY OF CONGRESS CATALOGING IN PUBLICATION DATA
Dexter, Catherine. Gertie's green thumb / by Catherine Dexter;
drawings by Ellen Eagle.   p. cm.   Summary: Eleven-year-old
Gertie, lover of plants and animals, finds a working wishbone in the
park and turns her family's home into a magical House of Nature.
    [1. Wishes—Fiction. 2. Nature—Fiction] I. Eagle, Ellen, ill. II.
Title.   PZ7.D 5387Ge 1983 [Fic] 94-20854 CIP AC
ISBN 0-688-13090-9 (pbk.)

First Beech Tree Edition, 1995. Published by arrangement with
Macmillan Publishing Company.
10 9 8 7 6 5 4 3 2 1

For Anna

    —C. D.

To my husband, Gordon Leavitt,
my parents, Arthur and Roslyn,
and my brother, David

    —E. E.

GERTIE'S GREEN THUMB

ONE

One cold November afternoon, Gertruda B. Darn-field came upon a working wishbone. She found it near a trash can in a public park. She didn't know there was anything special about it—it looked like a regular wishbone, but old and worn smooth. Gertie liked to collect things, so she put it into the zippered pocket of her parka, where it rattled around with two dry milkweed pods and several linty Chiclets. Then she forgot about it. The parka had a tear in the pocket, and the wishbone slipped through the tear and down into the jacket lining. In February, Gertie found it again. It poked her in the back as she sat on the floor, leaning against her bed.

"Ouch!" she cried. "What the—?" She took off her parka and felt the mysterious object through the cloth. She worked it around through the lining and drew it from her pocket. It was white, as hard as stone, and very light. The fork was perfectly symmetrical.

"Hey, I remember this thing," she said. "Maybe I can use it in the mouse house." Gertie had lined a shoe box with dried grass and sticks and feathers, intending to let a field mouse live in it. Field mice sometimes came into the basement, especially in the winter, and Gertie was sure she could catch one. Her mother had threatened to throw the box away. She said Gertie already had too many odds and ends in her room, and that, furthermore, her room was practically a health hazard—her shelves were so dirty she could grow potatoes on them.

Gertie's brother Thomas peered over her shoulder. He was twelve, and Gertie was eleven. "Where'd you get the wishbone?" he asked.

"Out by the trash can in the park. I found it a long time ago."

"Let's pull it and make a wish."

"I don't want to pull it. I'm going to use it for something."

"It'll just rot if you save it."

"No, it won't. It's all dried out."

"Chicken bones do rot," Thomas said.

"*I don't want to pull it.*"

Thomas caught the wishbone on one end and pulled. Gertie was still holding on to the other end. Of course it snapped, and Gertie was left holding the larger piece. She wailed, "Thomas, why can't you leave my stuff alone?"

Their squabbling brought their mother briskly up the stairs.

"He broke my wishbone!" Gertie cried.

"She only wants to keep things. She never wants to try them out."

"Hush!" their mother said. "Why must you always fight? When will you learn to settle things like civilized human beings?" She pulled open the hall closet and began fitting together various pieces of the vacuum cleaner. "You can help me clean up instead of fighting. Thomas, go to your room and make your bed. Gertie, please pick up your room. At least put your clothes away. Why do I have to ask you every single time?"

"Here, take your stupid old wishbone," Thomas said. He tossed the smaller end onto Gertie's bed and trudged away. Gertie picked up the bit of bone and tried to fit it to the part of the wishbone she was still holding.

"You know, it *is* true, Gertruda," her mother went on scolding. "You do keep things. You have a terrible habit of accumulating."

A *terrible habit of accumulating*. It made Gertie cringe to hear her mother's voice. Next, her mother would say that Gertie had to go through her room and throw out some of her stuff. Gertie had plants in paper cups and June bugs in jars, two bird's nests, and several snails in a saltwater fishbowl. She had started plants from lemon seeds, orange seeds, pumpkin seeds. Once she had stuck the top of a pineapple in a pot of dirt, and it grew for months. Her father had laughed when he saw the paper cups full of seedlings and the pineapple growing. "You have a green thumb," he said to her.

Gertie had looked in surprise at her skin-colored thumb.

"People used to say that about my grandmother, too," her father went on. "You have a talent for making things grow—green things like plants and flowers."

"Oh." Gertie had felt pleased. Her mother thought her talent was for making a mess. Gertie's room *was* rather cluttered. The paper cups and jars and makeshift cages were arranged mostly on the floor. The problem was, whenever her mother told her to please get rid of *some* things, Gertie would think about how the things would feel when they were thrown out, and that always made her stop. Then, before she knew it, she would come across another pair of June bugs and bring them home to keep the other ones company.

"I want to glue my wishbone first," said Gertie.

"For heaven's sake, you can't mend a wishbone! Just throw it away." Mrs. Darnfield turned on the vacuum cleaner and began nosing and bumping it into the corners of the hall, which in fact already looked quite clean. "And Gertie"—her mother yelled back over her shoulder— "you simply *must* throw out some of your plants. They're half-dead, anyway." The vacuum cleaner shrieked and

6

whined. Gertie hated the vacuum cleaner. It was ugly, and it was deafening, and it smelled bad, like old dust and electricity.

"I wish we could throw *that* thing away, and let this whole darned house be full of plants, and—and—" Gertie sputtered. She had forgotten that she was holding the wishbone.

As soon as the words were out of Gertie's mouth, her mother clicked off the vacuum cleaner with her toe and turned around. "What did you say?"

"I said, I wish this whole house was full of plants, and you would throw that thing away, and—" Gertie never finished her wish, because her mother suddenly looked so peculiar. Her mother was staring at the vacuum cleaner. "Why not?" she said.

So she did. She wrapped the cord around and around the vacuum cleaner and gathered up all the hideous tubes and wands and hairy little brushes.

Gertie watched in amazement. She followed her mother downstairs and watched her drop the entire vacuum cleaner into the trash can. "That's that!" Mrs. Darnfield said cheerfully.

Gertie wandered back to her room, stunned. She held the wishbone gingerly in her palm. It looked like any old bone—it gave off no sparks, it didn't tingle. In a daze, Gertie actually picked up her room. She scooped up the other piece of the wishbone and her parka and the clothes on the floor and stuffed everything into her closet.

After supper, Mr. Darnfield carried the trash can out to the street. He looked skeptical, but he was willing to do anything to preserve the family peace.

The next morning, the vacuum cleaner was taken away by the garbage truck.

"What's got into Mom?" Thomas whispered to Gertie as they watched the truck devour the contents of the trash can.

Gertie started to explain about the wishbone, but she wasn't sure if what had happened had really happened. All she said was, "Beats me."

At first, everything was the same as it had always been, only quieter.

After a couple of days, Gertie noticed that the floor was getting dusty awfully fast, and that she was leaving footprints on it. So was everyone else. Tracks went from the kitchen to the dining room and down the hall; tracks went up the front stairs, down the back stairs, and out to the pantry; and all kinds of tracks went in and out of the front door, the back door, the side door. To find out where anyone was, Gertie simply traced that person's footprints.

A few days after that, the dirt had piled up ankle deep,

and the Darnfields began to wear their boots around the house. When they spilled water, it made instant indoor mud puddles to splash through.

Mr. Darnfield changed into his hiking boots as soon as he got home from work. His boots were heavy, with round toes and dozens of hooks to lace. "They've always been my favorite shoes," he said, looking pleased. On snowy days he tracked in as much as he could.

One afternoon Gertie noticed a little green shoot in the corner of the dining room, under the south window. By the next day, fine little threads of grass were sprouting up everywhere, and soon the floor was carpeted with new green grass.

"Has Mom said anything to you about anything?" Thomas asked Gertie on Saturday morning. They were sitting at the breakfast table eating bowls of Cheerios. The table was covered with a thin coat of moss, and at one end, where it was sunny, two buttercups had just popped into bloom.

"About what?" Gertie blinked innocently and swallowed a spoonful of cereal.

"About this."

"Unh-unh." Gertie shook her head.

"Gertie. You know something."

"What's there to know? Mom just got tired of cleaning."

"If you don't tell me, you'll be sorry. I'll make you sorry."

"Aren't you glad you don't have to pick up anymore?"

Thomas *was* glad he didn't have to pick up, clean up, or straighten up. "Well, yeah," he said. "But it still seems kind of queer."

Gertie thought about how she would feel if their house suddenly collected dirt, sprouted grass, and began to grow green things all over, and she didn't know why, and her brother acted as if he knew why but wouldn't tell her. So she decided to tell him. "It was the wishbone," she said. "You remember I found that wishbone in my parka a couple of weeks ago? And you made me pull it? I got the wishing end, and by accident I made a wish, and I think the wish is coming true."

Thomas's eyes opened wide. "You mean the wishbone *worked*?"

"Yep. It actually worked."

"They're not supposed to. At least, I never heard of one working before. It's just a silly thing that you do."

Gertie shrugged.

"What'd you wish for?" Thomas asked.

"That Mom would throw the vacuum cleaner away. And we could have the whole house full of plants."

Thomas looked around at the green floor and flowering table. "You sure found the real thing," he said. "Have you still got it?"

"Yep."

"Where is it?"

"In my room."

"We ought to try it and see if it still works."

"Sure." Gertie tried to sound chipper. "I'll go get it later." She felt the smallest falter of doubt. She could definitely remember having it in her room, but she couldn't think just where she had put it.

Soon the Darnfields had kicked off their boots and were going barefoot in the fresh grass. It felt cool and silky beneath their feet. The grass kept growing thicker, and it spread everywhere: through the rooms on the first floor and up the stairs and all across the second floor. When Mrs. Darnfield saw how nicely the green things were growing, she decided to start an herb garden in one corner of the kitchen. (She said she had always believed in being adaptable.) She planted thyme and parsley and dill and sage. In other rooms, she planted tulip bulbs and lettuce and peas. Everything sprouted overnight and grew much faster than it would have in an ordinary garden. "You'd almost think those vegetables grew by magic," said Mrs. Darnfield. In a few days they were eating crisp new peas and beans.

Mr. and Mrs. Darnfield didn't know why all this had come about, but they didn't particularly care, because it was so very pleasant. "We all have green thumbs, and we never knew it," said Mr. Darnfield happily. The entire family was in the library garden on their hands and knees, picking lettuce leaves for a supper salad.

Mrs. Darnfield nodded her head. "I can't for the life of me think why I ever spent so much time cleaning the house."

Thomas gave Gertie a searching look. Gertie didn't meet his eyes. She lay down on her stomach instead and watched the blades of grass. She thought she could see them growing, right in front of her nose. A few ladybugs and two roly-polies came out of a tangle of underbrush. These were some of her favorites, and now she didn't even have to put them in jars.

In another week the Darnfields tossed out all their sofas and beds and tables and chairs and began to eat their meals as picnics. They brought their sleeping bags down from the attic and shook them out to air them. Each night they spread them on the grass at sunset and slept in them as soundly as if they had never seen a mattress in their lives.

With all the furniture gone, Mr. Darnfield saw that there was room for fruit trees. He decided to install an

orchard. (He had always loved home-improvement projects.) During school vacation, at the end of February, Mr. Darnfield took a few days off from his job, and the whole family set to work. They put skylights in the attic roof and cut away part of the first-floor ceilings to let the light through. Mr. Darnfield drove off to the nearest tree nursery in a rented truck. He brought back small peach trees and cherry trees, apricot trees and plum bushes. As soon as the trees were planted, they blossomed and put forth leaves. Birds peered in the windows. Mr. Darnfield raised them, and dozens of sparrows and robins and chickadees flapped across the sills, pecking and jostling for nesting spots. Smaller creatures hopped and slithered after them—squirrels, chipmunks, field mice, garter snakes. Mrs. Darnfield drew the line at that. She said she would have to keep the door shut against anything larger; there had to be some room left for the family. Nevertheless, she let a woeful pair of raccoons stay on the side porch, and she saved all the family's apple cores for them.

Soon it seemed to the Darnfields that they had always lived this way, and they could not imagine any other life.

TWO

ver since Gertie's wish had begun to work, the Darnfields had not had a moment to invite anyone over, even for a cup of coffee. Mr. and Mrs. Darnfield had been too busy to go to town meetings or school potluck suppers. They told their friends that they were working on their house. Everyone thought that meant putting up wallpaper or getting new furniture. Their neighbors had seen the beds and sofas on the sidewalk, waiting for the garbage truck, and they had heard the sawing and hammering. But the Darnfields' house sat back by itself on top of a hill, and no one could see anything unusual from the sidewalk. The greenery was barely beginning to sprout on the outside of the house.

Gertie's best friend, Allison Wood, had been away visiting her grandmother during the winter vacation. She telephoned Gertie the Saturday after she got back.

"You've got to come over!" Gertie told her. "We're growing grass in the dining room and beans in the pantry."

"Gertie! Are you tricking me?"

"No. Really. Wait till you see it. Ask your mom if you can come over."

Allison's mother sometimes disapproved of what Gertie and Allison did when they got together. Gertie was always carrying on strange, messy projects. Once she had had a worm farm, and another time she had asked for a Venus's-flytrap for her birthday. But Gertie was Allison's best friend. And so, even when she had her doubts, Mrs. Wood usually said yes when the two girls wanted to play together.

Gertie waited for Allison at the corner. Soon she saw Allison's red winter jacket bobbing up and down. The girls ran up the sidewalk, pushed through the Darnfields' front gate, and raced each other up the steps.

"Something is growing out of your front door!" Allison said.

"What'd I tell you?" Gertie laughed. Green leaves had poked through the mail slot in the front door, and more leaves curled in a little wreath around the doorbell button. The children opened the door and pushed through a tangle of honeysuckle vines. They shook several honeybees out of the vines. Something else darted by their ears. Was it red? Or emerald green?

"Hummingbirds," Gertie explained. "Nesting in the closet. The eggs are only as big as a dot."

They climbed up what had been the front stairs. Now there was a steep, narrow hill, carpeted in grass, with a bump where each stair used to be.

"Where'd your room go?" asked Allison. Through a thick mat of morning-glory vines Allison caught a glimpse of more tall grass and shrubs.

"This is it," Gertie said. They pushed through the vines. "See? I've got my own apricot tree. And there's a stream coming across here." She pointed to a shallow pool, which smelled rather swampy. From it, a trickle of water bubbled and flowed across the room and toward the outside wall. "We can go wading, if you want. There aren't any leeches, I already tried it. And look at the old dollhouse." The dollhouse, too, was overgrown with grass and miniature vines. A doll-sized cherry tree blossomed in its living room. "There's even a pond!" Allison said. In the dollhouse kitchen a pond sparkled in front of the dollhouse sink. The pond held a thimbleful of water. Blue violets grew on its shady banks. "And look here," Gertie whispered. She picked a grass stem and gently bent the dollhouse violets to one side. Beneath them slept four tiny frogs: a bullfrog, a smaller frog, and two smallest frogs, about a quarter of an inch long.

"How did you get all this in here?" Allison asked.

Gertie wanted to tell Allison the secret of the wishbone; but she also wanted to keep it a secret. So she half-explained. "It just started growing like this, and my mom decided to leave it the way it was."

Allison nodded. It was impossible to imagine *her* mother leaving it the way it was. "Where'd all your regular stuff go?" she asked.

"Some of it's back in there," Gertie said, waving her hand toward the closet. "By the way," she added, "if you happen to see an old chicken bone lying around, be sure to give it to me, okay?"

Allison poked her head around the corner of the closet doorway. She could see some puzzles and a record player balanced on a log. Gertie's clothes—two pairs of overalls, some socks, her parka, and her red velvet party dress—were hung among the branches of a new pear tree. Her sleeping bag was rolled up underneath. Beside the sleeping bag was a large white egg.

"Gertie! Look at this!" Allison picked it up and brought it out.

"Where did you find that?" Gertie shook it. It felt heavy.

"Do you think it's real?" asked Allison.

"It is," Gertie said. She lifted and lowered it a few times, weighing it in her hands. "Let's put it back where you found it. Maybe it'll hatch into a goose or a turkey or something."

20

Allison jiggled up and down on her toes. "Hey, this grass is soft!"

For a while they did gymnastics on the indoor lawn. Gertie practiced one-handed cartwheels, and Allison learned to do five backward somersaults in a row without getting dizzy afterward. Then they heard Gertie's father calling up to them: "I could use some extra hands! How about it?" The children looked over the banister and saw Mr. Darnfield carrying two large buckets into the front hall. The buckets had black letters printed on their sides: AGRICULTURAL EXTENSION SERVICE.

"What's in those?" Gertie called down, resting her elbows on a cascade of cucumber vines.

"Minnows. We're going to have fish." Mr. Darnfield was humming happily as he looked over sketches of the house. "Thomas and I are going to make two ponds. Then we'll stock them with fish. In the meantime, we have to keep the minnows in the bathtub."

Gertie and Allison helped Thomas and Mr. Darnfield carry the buckets into the house. They scooped the baby goldfish and trout out of the buckets with nets and slid them gently into the bathtub water. Then Gertie and Allison weeded the berry patch in the parlor, picked a few peaches, and sat down for a picnic of peaches and pears.

Gertie gave Allison a tiny green snake to take home in her pocket. It was the size of a thin earthworm and the color of the newest April grass. It was curled up into a perfect spiral. "You can keep him in a terrarium," she said. "You have to feed him flies and bugs, so tell your mom not to kill them but try to capture them alive, okay?"

Allison could hardly wait to tell her mother about it. "Mom, the Darnfields have a park in their house!" she said, as soon as she walked in the door. Her mother was busy lining up the books on the bookshelf so that they were all exactly the same distance from the edge.

"You mean a new play village?" asked Mrs. Wood. She liked to know about all the latest toys.

"No, it's real grass, all over the floor."

Probably a new acrylic rug, thought Mrs. Wood. Things were often exaggerated at the Darnfields'.

The Darnfields unrolled their sleeping bags early that evening. They decided to sleep in the study, where some new vines were crawling up the bookshelves. They were night-blooming vines. As the sun set, the white, trumpet-shaped blossoms opened. A breeze ruffled the grass, and down the hall the trout splashed musically in the bathtub.

Mr. Darnfield could remember hiking trips he had taken in the mountains when he was a boy, and each evening as he fell asleep he seemed to be camping again in the mountain air. Mrs. Darnfield began to dream of chickens. She had ordered a flock of chicks, because there is nothing like having fresh eggs every day.

Gertie heard Thomas rustling impatiently beside her. "Gert," he whispered. "You never did find that thing, did you?"

Gertie felt a tiny stab of guilt. "You mean the wishbone? I didn't really have time to look."

"When you find it, I want to have a turn with it. I'd like to wish for something. That would be fair."

"Yep. You can. It would be," Gertie replied.

The sweet smell from the glowing white flowers soon put them all to sleep.

THREE

ertie was naturally an early riser, even on weekends, but by the time she had rolled out of her sleeping bag the next morning, her parents were already at their chores. (All that could be seen of her brother was a large navy blue lump beside the bookcase.) Mr. Darnfield was tending to the beehives. Gertie could see him in the side yard, going back and forth between hives, wearing his bee veil. Cheerful hammering sounds came from behind the house. Her mother was starting to build a chicken coop in the backyard. She had left a note for Gertie in the kitchen, by the breadboard: "Working out back. Try new tea." The note was scribbled on a torn scrap of brown paper bag. A big glass jar held the dark tea leaves.

Gertie got her cup from its hook. It was a giant cup with bees and ants painted inside. The remnants of a gold line ran in little dashes around the rim. It had been Gertie's ever since she was a baby, a gift from her greatgrandmother Lloyd, to whom it had been given when *she* was a baby. It was not the thin sort of china that breaks if you bang it even once against something, but was made of thick, hearty stuff that felt heavy and solid in her hand. It had survived any number of knocks and had even been dropped. Of course, if she dropped it now, it would just bounce off the mossy floor.

Gertie filled the kettle with cold water and put it on the back of the wood stove, where it would heat up faster. She opened the big glass jar and scooped out a spoonful of tea. It smelled delicious, like cinnamon. She poured the tea leaves into the cup. She usually made her tea very strong, and then added two ice cubes to cool it. She liked it with plenty of milk and honey. The end of a loaf of golden raisin bread stood on the breadboard. She sliced two thick pieces. That left only a tiny curled heel, which she set down for Hopper, the most outgoing of the sparrows. A sparrow was not Gertie's idea of an interesting bird, but she couldn't exactly choose which birds came to stay and which did not. Hopper, if he was not exotic, was unfailingly loyal. The butter dish was empty. No matter—there was a new jar of honey. She spread it over the bread, crushing down the bits of honeycomb. Then she set the two pieces side by side, ready to eat, while she waited for the water to boil.

The kettle made plinking noises as the steam began to rise. Gertie stretched. She had plans for today. As soon as she had finished her breakfast, she was going to search everywhere for the wishbone. Then, she would help her mother build the chicken coop. Gertie was just about to take the kettle off the stove when all the window frames in the kitchen rattled. The walls creaked, and the floor jiggled. Several loud thumps shook the side of the house. Either they were having an earthquake, or something large was struggling to get into the side porch. Gertie heard some snorts and a long, shivery blowing out of air. It sounded like an animal breathing.

Gertie tiptoed through the back hall to the side porch door. She opened the door silently, trying to keep as much of herself out of sight as she could. She peered around the woodwork and just missed bumping into an enormous brown velvet nose. The nose was the nearest part of a long brown velvet head, with eyes as big as her hands. The eyes looked directly at her, and she saw that the head continued outside the screen and became branches or something.

"Oh!" Gertie said, in a tiny voice.

The giant eyes closed a bit, as if the animal wished to appear less frightening. It was shaped like a horse or a deer, but with larger shoulders. The branches on its head were antlers. They looked webbed, and they were rounded on the ends rather than pointed. The animal had poked its head through one of the empty spaces where a screen was missing, and then had not been able to pull its head back out. At last Gertie recognized it. She had seen one once, stuffed, in a museum.

"You're a moose!" she said. The heavy-lidded eyes blinked in what seemed to be a polite "yes."

"Now, I'll be right back. Don't go anywhere." Gertie began to dance around excitedly on the grass of the porch floor. "My mother and father can help you. Boy, will they be surprised!"

She ran pell-mell back through the house, calling, "It's a moose, would you believe? A moose! Mom! Pop!"

Mrs. Darnfield came in when she heard Gertie calling. She had thought the thumping noise was Mr. Darnfield. Mr. Darnfield had just come into the front hall and was taking off his bee veil. He had thought the thumping noise was Mrs. Darnfield. They looked at each other skeptically. A moose? A few blades of grass, an indoor orchard and whatnot, that was one thing. But a moose is a large animal with a will of its own.

"Thomas!" Gertie bellowed, to wake him. "Now we've got a moose!"

Thomas sat straight up, unzipped his sleeping bag, and wriggled out. "A what?"

"Are you quite sure?" asked Gertie's mother.

"We have to figure out what he likes to eat," Gertie said. She led them back to the porch.

"It *is* a moose," said Mr. Darnfield. "And look at how tired he is." Mr. Darnfield set to work at once to loosen two or three screens and free the moose's head. He already liked its silent, sturdy presence. Privately, he preferred an animal with some size to it, rather than those small ones always scampering and slithering around.

"I think we should name him. I know a good name: Melrose," Gertie said.

Melrose watched patiently as Mr. Darnfield grunted and groaned and turned red trying to loosen the window. Gertie and Thomas helped to pry the frame away. At last the moose's head was free. He backed up and nodded, to show he was satisfied.

"That's better, old boy, isn't it," said Mr. Darnfield, patting him on the nose. Melrose gave a snort that plainly meant he agreed.

Mr. Darnfield spent the rest of that morning building a shed for Melrose, a lean-to against the back of the house where there was a double window. Melrose could put his head through the wide window to eat indoors, yet still stand outdoors, where he had room for his long legs and big shoulders. When the lean-to was finished, Mr. Darnfield led Melrose into it. Melrose quickly ate up everything within reach—leaves, twigs, buds, everything his rubbery lips could slurp up. His favorites were

28

moss and the juicy plants that grew with their roots in water. He liked water lilies best of all.

Late that afternoon Thomas and Gertie stood on benches in the dim light of the lean-to and brushed Melrose's coat. There were bald patches in his fur and rough spots full of burrs. He stood very still, because he enjoyed the brushing.

"Now aren't you glad I made you break the wish-bone?" Thomas said. "If I hadn't, we'd've never had a pet moose."

"He's not actually a pet, yet," Gertie said. "Besides, Thomas, I was the one who made the wish."

"Well." Thomas couldn't think of an answer, and any-way, the rhythm of the brushing was taking away his inclination to fight.

"What if more animals come?" Thomas went on. "What animals exactly did you wish for?"

"Nothing special. Wishbones don't seem to be very exact. I wished for plants all over the house, and for Mom to throw out the vacuum cleaner, and for—and for—hey! You want to know something?"

"What?"

"I never finished my wish. I started the wish, and I never got to the end of it."

"You mean you left your wish dangling?"

"I guess. I never got to the end of what I was saying."

"Gertie! That means we don't have to worry about the wishbone working again. You can finish the wish you started!"

"How do you know?"

"Well, magic things don't let you down in midair. They might not do what you thought you wanted them to do, but they don't cheat."

"Right." Gertie wasn't sure, but Thomas was usually good at figuring things out. "So I wonder if I can just say the rest of the wish right now. If I knew what I wanted it to be."

"I think you have to be *holding* the wishbone."

"You mean the wishing end of the wishbone."

"That's right."

They brushed in silence for a few minutes. At last Gertie put down her brush. "I'm going upstairs to look one more time."

"What for?"

"The wishbone."

"You mean you really can't find it?"

"I'm pretty sure I left it in my closet."

Thomas put his brush down, too. "I'll come up and help you."

It was growing dark, and Gertie's room was full of

dusky green twilight. Their eyes gradually got used to the half-dark.

"It's getting kind of swampy up here," Thomas said.

"I like it this way," said Gertie. "I turned all my water snails loose, and there are frogs all over the place, little tiny ones, about an inch long. I mean, there used to be. There don't seem to be as many now. That's queer."

Gertie shuffled through the potato vines on her shelves and scuffed her toes through the grass. Nothing. She got down on her hands and knees in the closet and combed the grass with her fingers. Something sharp dug into her finger. She jumped up, shaking her hand. "What's in there?" she said, backing away. A small, lizardlike creature came out of the closet, turning its head from side to side and blinking. It was shiny black, with yellow bands around its middle. It had fine, scaly skin and round, amber-colored eyes. It opened its mouth and showed tiny white pointed teeth.

"Is that some kind of a lizard?" Thomas asked.

The creature, which was nine or ten inches long, slithered toward Gertie. Gertie bent down, rubbing the bite marks on her hand. "Up close it doesn't look like a regular lizard," she said doubtfully. "It's more like a miniature alligator."

"Watch out! It's hungry!" Thomas scrambled through the bushes to the safety of the hall.

"What do you think it eats?" Gertie asked.

"Meat."

Gertie skipped through the narrow gap in the wall of bushes. The alligator scurried back to the edge of the pond and snapped at water beetles.

"We better feed it," Gertie said. "Maybe that's what happened to all the frogs." The thought made her feel a little squeamish.

The children ran downstairs. The grass in the pantry was as high as their heads. "Pop still hasn't mowed the kitchen," Gertie grumbled. They swordfished their way through the weeds and pussy willows and pulled open a cupboard door. The shelves were getting awfully bare. Mrs. Darnfield scarcely ever had to buy any food now. Gertie found a lone can of tuna fish and opened it. She shook the tuna fish out onto a leftover styrofoam tray from the supermarket.

They carried the tray back upstairs and set it down just inside Gertie's room. The alligator ran over. It ate all the tuna fish, and the styrofoam tray as well. Then it stretched out beneath a window. Just over its head, the evening star was visible, shining in the deep blue dusk. The creature's eyes closed, and a wisp of a happy smile drifted around the corners of its mouth.

"You know what I think?" Thomas said to Gertie.

"What?"

"If this thing's been up here, it probably ate the wishbone."

"Why would it do that?"

"Because it's a carnivore."

"But would a wishbone taste good, even to a carnivore?"

"To an alligator, it's probably like a pretzel."

"Then how will we change things back?" Gertie asked.

"You can't," Thomas answered. "It takes magic to undo magic."

"Maybe we won't need to undo it," Gertie said. "It's going all right so far."

"Supper, children!" Mrs. Darnfield called from below. "Will one of you please come down and set the blanket?"

"Good night, Al," Gertie whispered. She gave the alligator a little salute as they went downstairs.

Gertie pulled out the Sunday picnic blanket from the china cabinet and spread it on the dining room floor.

"What a nice spot!" said Mrs. Darnfield. She carried in a tray with a bean sprout omelet and some burned toast and a large bowl of green leaves. "Sorry about the toast. I was checking on Melrose. He has a delightful disposition. He's very calm." They stretched out on the blanket and began to eat.

"What's in that?" asked Gertie suspiciously, peering over the rim of the bowl of leaves.

"Beautiful fresh spinach," her mother replied.

"Yuck," said Gertie.

"It's good for you," said her father. He crunched dutifully on the spinach. Sometimes, secretly, he longed for the good old days of regular lettuce.

"I hate spinach."

"What a treat! It's as fresh as fresh can be."

"That makes it worse, Mom. Can I have something else? Please? Can I have a carrot instead?"

Her mother sighed. "Oh, all right," she said. "But you'll have to pull it yourself."

A homely brown toad hopped to the edge of their blanket and looked up at them with luminous yellow eyes.

"Here's a fine fellow," said Gertie's father, a trifle disconcerted.

"I've noticed that toad before," said Mrs. Darnfield. "He always comes by as we're finishing our meals. He likes to wait for flies. Isn't it nice to be so well taken care of?"

FOUR

Mr. Tannenbaum, the bus driver, blew the horn of his bus. The Darnfield children were late again. This was the third day in a row. They had never been a problem before. They used to be neat children, too. That was the sign of a good home, Mr. Tannenbaum thought: hair brushed, clothes pressed, lunchboxes clean. Now they looked—well, they looked weird, that was the only word for it. Was there something about the end of winter? Did the Darnfields already have spring fever?

Mr. Tannenbaum blew his horn again. Nobody came. He drove around the corner and halfway up the street, to the Darnfields' gate. He wasn't supposed to do that, because it took extra time; but waiting took extra time, too. Mr. Tannenbaum leaned over the steering wheel of his bus and craned his neck to look up at the Darnfields' house. His eyes opened wide.

The house had sprouted. Green branches were sticking out through the windows. He saw red balls on the branches. Could they be apples? How could apples be growing on trees in March? Come to think of it, how could apple trees be growing through a skylight? Why weren't the leaves frozen? Why were there leaves at all? Green vines were strung across the front of the house. Where was the front door?

His two passengers popped out of the vines where the front door used to be and tumbled down the steps to the bus. A ripple of whispers and giggles ran from the front row of seats to the back. Gertie's hair stuck out like a curly bush, with tendrils going every which way. She and Thomas had worn the same clothes for several days, and by now their shirts and overalls smelled smoky and mossy, like a wood fire. Burrs and twigs and fuzzy weed-heads clung to their pant legs.

"Are you guys living in a field, or what?" called out Gus Grand. "Even my dog gets brushed!" Everybody laughed as Gertie and Thomas climbed on the bus.

"Do we look funny?" Thomas asked. Thomas and Gertie looked at each other, and they began to laugh, too.

Gertie's teacher, Mrs. Axel, was worried. At lunchtime, she and Thomas's teacher, Miss Wind, sat together in the teachers' lounge and discussed the Darnfield children. They had both been thinking the children looked neglected, and they wondered if they ought to ask the principal about it. Perhaps the Darnfield parents were ill. The children had not had baths, and they were not acting like their normal selves. They didn't pay attention to their classwork, and they always had their minds on something else.

In the lunchroom yesterday, Mrs. Axel had seen Gertie open her lunchbox, and a brown snake had slithered out. It slid right over the waxed paper and across the tabletop. All the children at her table had squealed. Gertie had grabbed it and popped it back beneath the tin lid. But still! A snake in with your sandwich? It made Mrs. Axel shiver.

The children didn't seem unhappy, though. That was the strange part. They looked too happy. They acted as if they were sharing a joke. Miss Wind and Mrs. Axel decided to send notes home.

Mrs. Darnfield got the notes, but she never had a chance to read them, for the chickens were delivered that same afternoon. The delivery man brought an enormous brown carton into the front hall and set it down on the grass. "It's very light. You can carry it to your coop or whatever yourself." He took a moment to look around him as he flipped through his receipt book for the bill. "You could just let them loose right here, couldn't you?" he said, half-joking.

"We could, but if it turns out that we have a fox, they won't mix very well," said Mrs. Darnfield.

The delivery man looked surprised. He didn't make any more suggestions.

Mrs. Darnfield unstapled the lid of the box and lifted it off. Gertie heard the noise of soft peeping. She peered over the edge of the box and saw dozens of fuzzy brown chicks darting around on the bottom. "Beautiful, aren't they?" Mrs. Darnfield looked over Gertie's shoulder. "Let's take them right out to their new home."

All Thursday morning it snowed, and school was closed. After lunch, the snow stopped falling, and Gertie could hear Melrose stamping his feet and bumping against the walls of his lean-to. "He wants to get out," she said to Thomas. She was standing in the doorway to the library, which was as close as Thomas would allow her to come. Dozens of stones lay in an arc across the far corner of the room. Thomas was building a bridge to cross the stream. He had collected a heap of round stones, all the same size, and had drawn a diagram of an arched bridge. He had laid out all the stones in the order in which he thought he would use them. Now he was going to figure out how to stick them together.

"This is probably Melrose's favorite weather," Gertie went on. "Let's go let him out."

"Okay." Thomas got to his feet and surveyed the layout. "Don't mess any of these up, will you?"

They pulled on their jackets and boots and went out to unlatch the lean-to. The yard was full of wet, heavy snow that began to melt as soon as the sun shone. The last clouds blew away and left a bright blue sky. Melrose shook himself with pleasure and tramped out to the back fence. He looked handsome, even majestic, as he passed beneath the snowy branches. Children pulling sleds began to come up the street. They stopped as soon as they saw the moose ambling down the Darnfields' hill. Melrose, who had a friendly and inquisitive nature, walked over to the sidewalk to have a look at them.

"What is that thing, anyway?" asked Sam Snyder.

"A moose," Gertie answered.

"Where'd you get him?"

"We don't know."

"You don't know?"

Gertie shrugged her shoulders.

"How can you have a moose and not know where he came from? You just woke up one morning and you had a moose?"

"We think he's from Canada," Gertie said. "But my mother isn't sure. You don't order them from Sears, Roebuck, you know."

Sam's admiring eyes took in Melrose's mighty legs,

his thick neck, his large but sensitive nose. "Can we pet him?" Sam asked.

The children reached up, and Melrose nudged their mittens.

"Allison says you've got other stuff in your house," Peggy Brown said. "Like animals living right in with you."

"I bet it stinks in there," said Gus Grand.

"We did let a few in," Thomas said. "We'll show you around later. Does anybody want a ride on Melrose?"

More children arrived and wanted to know about Melrose. Melrose took them for short rides up and down the hill. Soon the sunshine had attracted adults, too. Some of them immediately began to worry about the safety of the children. Others gawked at the house. Green leaves and vines full of spring buds, all sparkling with snow, curled and sprang from every crack and corner—around the door handles, beneath the eaves, around the chimney, and up the gutters. Tendrils drooped from the tops of the windows in thick fringes.

Drivers of passing cars slammed on their brakes when they caught sight of the Darnfields' house. They thought they were seeing a giant potted plant stuck in a snow-bank. A traffic jam developed.

"I hope this isn't starting a trend," said Mrs. Darn-field.

"You want to go for a ride on a what?" Mrs. Wood was busy unloading her dishwasher, and she was sure she must have heard Allison wrong.

"A moose. Gertie and Thomas have a moose. So can I go?"

"What next?" Mrs. Wood sighed. "I suppose this is some kind of early April Fools' joke. This time I'm coming along with you. I think I need to have a few words with Gertie's mother." The Darnfields were beginning to try Mrs. Wood's patience—always these wild tales.

Allison and Mrs. Wood came around the corner of the Darnfields' hill. Mrs. Wood squinted and began to walk faster. There certainly was something large and brown and antlered going up the hill there. Mrs. Wood walked even faster. There certainly was something green and twiny and viny growing out of the house. Mrs. Wood ran up the snowy steps. She batted aside the strands of honeysuckle without even noticing them and rang the front bell. Mrs. Darnfield answered the door. Mrs. Wood walked straight in. Her high-heeled boots sank into the spongy grass. She suddenly realized that she was inside the Darnfields' house, and it was strange—so strange that she could not think of anything to say. Every one of her tried-and-true remarks flapped through her mind like

43

a pack of worn cards, and none of them held an appropriate sentence.

"We've made some changes here in the house," Mrs. Darnfield said. She waved her hand carelessly at the lemon grove. A great blue parrot flew from a corner tree and sat on Mrs. Wood's crocheted hat. Its black claws scratched her scalp. "*Speak!*" the parrot squawked.

"But this is—most extraordinary—so unusual, not the least what anyone else I know is doing—" Mrs. Wood gasped, still unable to extract her heels from the topsoil.

Then Mrs. Wood had an inspiration. For Mrs. Wood was not an ordinary mother, like yours and mine. She was like five mothers, or ten or twenty, all rolled into one. Mrs. Wood had been born with the urge to manage things, and whatever strayed into her path was managed, whether it wanted to be or not. She loved committees, meetings, events, tours, and arrangements. Now she forgot that her boots were stuck. She even forgot that she disliked parrots sitting on her head.

"Oh, *do* show me around!" she said, changing to her sweetest voice. She gave up on her boots, stepped out of them, and soon was strolling through daisy fields and skirting frog ponds. "*Simply marvelous! What a find! Nature at its purest!*"

When she had seen all the rooms, Mrs. Wood said to Gertie's mother, "You know, this house could make you famous. You are going to be swamped with visitors once everyone hears about this—this—new decorating scheme. You will be overrun with people! The house will be ruined," she added.

"What an awful thought!" Mrs. Darnfield said. "But I'm sure you're wrong. We are just quietly going about our business. People won't really be interested."

Mrs. Wood shook her head. "They will, they will. You'll see. And when they are, you come straight to me." She squeezed Mrs. Darnfield's arm, as if they had always been the closest of friends. "Now I must be off. Allison, you go on out now and take a turn on the moose!"

She left in a state of calculating rapture.

FIVE

The next morning Allison's mother knocked on their door at dawn. She was carrying a large sign on which she had lettered, in beautiful, neat capitals:

HOUSE OF NATURE
OPEN TO THE PUBLIC
TUESDAYS, THURSDAYS, 1:00–5:00
SATURDAYS, ALL DAY, DAWN TO DUSK

ADMISSION: ADULTS, THREE DOLLARS

CHILDREN, ONE DOLLAR

CHILDREN UNDER THREE, TEN CENTS

DOGS AND CATS, FIFTY CENTS

"Do you like it?" she asked. Before they could answer, she took the sign to the front gate and hammered it into the ground beside a heap of melting snow.

"I saw all the crowds yesterday, and I thought this was the least I could do to help. I myself enjoy crowds of people. If you like, you can leave everything to me. I would be happy to manage tours of the House of Nature."

Mr. and Mrs. Darnfield felt a little doubtful, but Mrs. Wood seemed to know what she was doing. Besides, the sign worked. It was Friday, and no one came.

"Now, why don't you show me where everything is," Mrs. Wood went on. "Then I can think up the best path for the tourists." She went eagerly from one room to the next. She broad-jumped over the streams and pushed through the blackberry prickles. She was wearing a pair of high-topped basketball sneakers so that she would not get stuck in the mud again. When she rounded the last corner, she came to Melrose's window. Melrose was in it, chewing a bit of water weed.

"My word! It comes inside, too?" Mrs. Wood took several steps backward. She stared, horrified, at Melrose's enormous eyes and patchy fur. "Well! He's ecologically out of place, I do believe." She crisply turned her back.

Melrose blinked and went on chewing.

After she had looked at everything on the first floor, Mrs. Wood chose a comfortable spot for herself in the clover at the foot of the front stairs. She drew a small clipboard and a notepad from her purse and began to scribble notes and sketch floor plans. "Let me see . . . guide ropes for tourist paths, signs to say No Picking, admission tickets, cash registers . . . Good. That's everything. Oh, this is going to be wonderful!"

At first, the Darnfields tried to accept the tourists with good grace. It made them happy to hear everyone admiring the house. Every corner glowed with fresh green leaves and was fragrant with flowers and fruits and vegetables. There was a Florida room with orange trees, a prairie room with wheat, a room full of herbs and roses, a tropical room with a coconut tree. Thomas had finished his stone bridge, and it looked handsome in the library corner by the lettuce patch. It was strong enough to hold adults, if they crossed it one at a time.

But it was inconvenient, dropping everything at one o'clock on Tuesday, and one o'clock on Thursday, and all day long on Saturday. Mrs. Wood wanted Mr. Darnfield to help with the crowds, so he had to ask his company for permission to leave work at noon on Tuesdays and Thursdays. His company said yes, but they didn't like it much. And the Darnfields had to keep up with their gardening chores, even while the tourists came through. Soon the Darnfields were stared at almost as much as their house was. Mr. Darnfield especially disliked the moment when Mrs. Wood opened the front door, parted the vines, and called out to the waiting crowd: "Welcome to the House of Nature!" She would step to one

side, her hostess badge twinkling in the sun, and the people would come pouring in. Mr. Darnfield would look up and nod and smile faintly as the mothers and fathers and mobs of children tramped past him.

"Ooooh, look, he's feeding a porcupine!"

"How's he keep from getting stuck, Ma? How does he?"

The parents were too busy to answer. They were marveling at the archways leading to meadows, the polished woodwork framing herb gardens.

"Come along, now, come along," Mrs. Wood would say. "Let's move on, or we'll miss the buttercups! The day lilies are just opening! And a family of snapping turtles is sunning themselves in the parlor!"

Mr. Darnfield was glad when they had gone on to the next room and weren't looking at him any more.

Gertie didn't mind the people coming through or looking at her, but she did mind having to tidy up the ponds and meadows all the time. When it got too noisy downstairs, Gertie sneaked up to her room, out of hearing range. She would check on her box turtles, or count frogs, or she would sit down quietly beside the alligator while it slept. Its black skin had intricate crisscross patterns, and yellow marks decorated its sides, like dabs from a tempera brush. Every day it looked a little larger than it had the day before.

Soon the money from admission tickets had piled up. Mr. Darnfield spent some of it on a waterfall. He had stonemasons come and build it under the front staircase. Then he called a plumber to install more drains and pipes, so that the household ponds were always full of bubbling fresh water. The Darnfields regularly caught their supper in the ponds after the last tourist had gone home. That was the best moment of the day: the door closed, the noise of voices faded, and the house was theirs again. A few birds would hop across the still grass, and once more they could hear the gentle splashing of the waterfall.

One Tuesday in May, Mrs. Wood arrived an hour early. She was very excited. "The TV station is coming! With cameras! We're going to be on TV!" She shouted this out to the house in general, as if she hoped the animals themselves would ruff up their coats and put bits of straw behind their ears.

At two o'clock sharp, the camera crew came in, trailing thick electric cables and holding up blinding lights. They made a film of a friendly, talkative man talking. He stood in front of Mr. Darnfield and talked while Mr. Darnfield moved rocks around the waterfall; and he stood to one side and talked while Gertie and Thomas and Allison fished in the ponds; and he stood close to the camera and talked while Mrs. Darnfield fed the chickens from bags of grain.

Gertie could hardly wait to see how she would look. After supper, the Darnfields went to Allison's house and watched themselves on the Woods' television set. Mr. and Mrs. Darnfield thought they looked very unimportant, compared with the talkative man, and their house did not look like anything special. They could have been standing in any old greenhouse anywhere.

Gertie was delighted. She thought they all looked just like their real selves, even when they were glancing nervously into the camera. There Gertie was herself, digging in the bank for fishing worms; the camera showed the heart-shaped patch on the knee of her overalls.

And there was Thomas, making the funny face he always made when he first cast his fishing line into the water; and Mrs. Darnfield could be heard saying, "Here chick, here chick," just as she always did when she fed the chickens.

"Can we watch the late news, too? Maybe we'll be on again," Thomas said.

A few days later, more television teams came, this time from the networks that showed evening news all over the country. The next week the Darnfields saw themselves on the national news broadcast for seven minutes. So did sixty million other people.

After that, everything changed. The Darnfields got dozens of telephone calls and hundreds of letters. The post office had to rent a special room for the Darnfields' mail and hire an extra postman to stack the letters. There were too many to deliver, so the post office sent an empty mail truck around for the Darnfields, and they were delivered to their mail, rather than the other way around.

Then one day a special letter came all by itself. A sleek black limousine parked in front of the house, and a man in a uniform got out. He handed Mr. Darnfield a thick ivory envelope with a huge seal stamped on its flap. It was from the president of the United States. The president had been watching the news, and he had just seen the story about the Darnfields. He was very fond of gardens, and he wanted to visit the Darnfields himself. He was going to come next week.

"Wow!" said Gertie and Thomas together.

SIX

Early on the morning of the president's visit, the Darnfields and Mrs. Wood and Allison and the mayor of the city and every other important person in town gathered in the park to wait. The president's helicopters were going to land on the thick grass of the soccer field, and then everyone would walk from the park to the Darnfields' house. One family had painted a king-sized sheet with green letters three feet high: WELCOME MR. PRES. They had spread it on the ground so that the president could read it from the air. They stood on the edges of the sheet, to keep it from blowing away.

The Darnfields had pruned, clipped, raked, watered, and polished every leaf and twig in the entire house. They had laid out a special path, spreading it with moss so that it felt like a Persian carpet. If they could have blown clouds to order, they'd have done that, too: a few white puffs to float in the blue sky.

At last they heard the fleet of helicopters droning in

the distance. Sunlight flashed off silvery sides and tails. The helicopters moved closer to earth and dropped to the ground with a deafening racket. The doors opened, and twelve men in navy blue suits came out. A short man emerged from the last helicopter. When he reached the welcoming line, Gertie nudged Thomas. "That's him," she whispered.

The president shook hands first with Mr. Darnfield, and then with Mrs. Darnfield, and then he shook hands with Gertie. Gertie felt as if a line of trumpets were blowing a golden fanfare just for her. The president shed importance all around him like light from a lamp. She glowed as the photographers aimed their cameras at her and the president. The president moved on to shake Thomas's hand, and then Mrs. Wood's hand, and then the next person's. Gertie felt the glow of importance fade and move to her left, down the line of people.

The entire group walked together from the park to the House of Nature. The sidewalks had been swept, and cords were strung along the sides to keep back the crowds of curious neighbors. Mrs. Wood had run ahead and was waiting for them at the top of the stairs. She was wearing the red, white, and blue dress she saved for patriotic occasions. It rippled in the breeze like a flag. She also wore a pair of boots.

"You should leave your shoes by the door," Mrs. Wood said. "Otherwise they'll get too muddy. We have rented rubber boots for everyone to put on while you tour the house." The president bent down and took off his shoes and tucked them under the hedge in the front hall. So did the twelve secret-service men, the reporters, the important townspeople, and everybody else. A photographer darted up and took a picture of the president's shoes. Dozens of pairs of rubber boots lined the hallway in rows, going from small to large. The president chose a pair and put them on. Everyone else put on boots, too.

"We will begin with the simple flowers of the North American meadow. . . ." Mrs. Wood's voice rose on ringing notes as she disappeared into the library. She and Mr. and Mrs. Darnfield led the president on the Grand Tour, past the fresh-water pond and the salt-water pond, the white sand beach and the muddy flats. The president went through the gardens. He ate peaches from the orchard and picked apples from the trees that grew through the skylights. He stepped over chipmunks; he waited for a box turtle to cross his path; he moved cautiously past a family of skunks.

The children trailed far behind. After the president had seen the last leafy corner, he turned and waited for

Gertie and Thomas to catch up. "Your house is terrific," he told them. "I wish I had brought my grandchildren. They would have loved it. Before we go, is there anything special you would like to show me?"

"Would you like to see my alligator?" Gertie asked, without thinking first.

"Well—er—of course!" The president gave a nervous laugh.

Mrs. Wood, Mrs. Darnfield, and Mr. Darnfield all exclaimed at once—

"Alligator?"

"What alligator?"

"There's no alligator!"

Gertie led them up the stairs and across the second-floor landing to her room. She pushed the morning-glory vines to one side. "He's probably asleep," she said. She went through the doorway and walked around the edge of the pond. To her surprise, the alligator was not there.

Where could he have gone? Gertie felt a nervous pinprick in her stomach. Al had never left her room before. An alligator was not a good animal to have turn up unexpectedly. "Well, that's too bad," she said, not wanting to alarm anyone. "The alligator's gone in for now. Maybe I can find a toad instead. You could take a toad back to your grandchildren. I'll look in my closet. There usually are lots in there. A toad makes a nice pet, if you take care of it."

"A toad?" the president repeated.

Gertie searched her closet shelves for a toad that was just the right size. "You better take two," she said, emerging with a pair of fat ones. "Keep them damp. We'll give you some moss and stuff in a plastic bag."

A secret-service man took one of the toads, and another secret-service man took the other.

"Now, then. We have something to give to you, too," the president announced. "Let's go back downstairs, and I'll show you what it is."

One of the president's aides was standing by the front door. He was holding a stack of dark velvet boxes. The president opened the two boxes on top and took out wide red satin ribbons. A gold medal gleamed on each ribbon. He put them around Mr. and Mrs. Darnfield's necks. "I am proud to give you the United States' highest citizen award, the Medal of Natural Achievement." He opened a third box. "And to Mrs. Wood, we present the Medal of Tireless Efforts."

Everyone clapped. The Darnfields turned pink with embarrassment as the ribbons were put around their necks, and Mrs. Wood turned red with pride.

"And what a wonderful young citizen you are," the

president said, turning to Gertie. He put a green ribbon around her neck. Her medal read: "Outstanding Young Citizen." He did exactly the same thing for Thomas and for Allison.

"Thank you," said Gertie. She turned up her medal. It had an eagle engraved on the front. She turned it over and found her name engraved on the back.

The secret-service men clicked on their belt radios and began to give orders. "Time to leave!" "The helicopters are waiting!" "Let's go!" The first secret-service man reached under the hedge to pick out his shoes. Instead, he touched a cool, scaly head. Al stood beneath the shelter of the low branches and looked out shyly. His mouth was closed, and a shoelace trailed from one corner of his jaw. Then he came cautiously into the hallway, until his full length was stretched before them, so dark and gleaming that he looked almost purple.

"I told you we had one!" Gertie cried. "Now you can see him!" But the others were not so delighted as she was.

"So there is an alligator!"

"My word, it's eaten someone!"

"Anyone we know?"

"It ate both my shoes!"

Some people tried to run away, and others tried to snatch back their shoes. Al was frightened by the noise.

Gertie thought she saw him dart into a patch of reeds behind the waterfall; but he went so quickly, she couldn't be sure.

The president put up his hands and called for quiet. "Please calm down, everyone, please calm down. The alligator has gone. Now, is anyone missing?"

They counted themselves and checked for all their friends. No one was missing. The pile of shoes beneath the hedge was much smaller than it had been, though. Only a few sneakers and three pairs of rubber overshoes were left.

"The alligator seems to be especially fond of leather," the president said. "Well, all I can say is, we have given him a banquet! We have to leave now, to keep to our schedule. Fortunately we are all wearing boots. I hope the Darnfields won't mind if we borrow them to go home in. We'll send them back right away. And now, we must say good-by to the Darnfields. Thank you, Gertruda, for this extra—er—treat."

The visitors waved good-by and tried to be polite about the shoes. As they made their way down the front steps, Allison raced out from the kitchen with the forgotten plastic bags of moss. She tugged at the sleeve of the last secret-service man: "Here, give these to the president! They're for his toads."

The Darnfields and the Woods followed the group to

the park, where the helicopters were waiting. The visitors disappeared into the helicopters. The blades whirled faster and faster until they were invisible. Gertie saw the president looking out the window at them. He held his hands cupped with the palms toward the glass, showing them a brownish blob. It had to be the toads.

Gertie and Allison and Thomas stood side by side and waved. Their hair and clothes were pressed back by the winds when the helicopters lifted up. Gertie felt a momentary sadness as the helicopters dwindled in the sky. She thought it unlikely that they would ever see the president again, and they were just starting to be friends.

Before the sky was completely empty, they turned and went back in for lunch.

The president's thank-you letter came twenty-four hours later. It was beautifully typed in black letters on thick stationery. The presidential seal glowed in blue at the top of the page.

> For our wonderful visit to your House of Nature, we send our warmest thanks. We admired your handiwork so much that we are going to install an indoor-outdoor room at the White House.
>
> > Very truly yours,
> > The President of the United States

The envelope was lumpy. Gertie shook it, and a wad of yellow, lined paper fell out. It was a note from Martha and Lawrence, the president's grandchildren, written in purple marker in very nice printing:

Thank you very much for the toads. The toads doing fine. When can we come to see you ourselves?

At the bottom were drawings of two children and two toads, with names printed beneath: Kitty and Peter.

An enormous box was delivered shortly afterward. In it were the dozens of pairs of rubber boots.

Two weeks later a beautiful leaflet came in the mail. It was full of color photographs of the new White House American Nature Room. The room had a large assortment of native American animals and plants. The animals had to be in cages, but the cages were cleverly designed, so that visitors hardly noticed them. Stars were painted on the ceiling. During the day a large light shone down, like the sun; at night the painted stars glowed in the dark. Thousands of tourists came through the room, and every night the First Grandchildren slept there in their sleeping bags. The room was called the Whittemore Room, in honor of one of America's greatest naturalists.

Mrs. Wood was thrilled. "I told you you'd be famous!" she said. She felt that she, too, had been placed right up on the historical shelf next to Whittemore.

Mr. and Mrs. Darnfield said that they hoped the new Whittemore Room would attract all the tourists away from the House of Nature. Then they could go back to living in peace and quiet.

Gertie had never heard of Whittemore, and privately she felt a little disappointed that the room had not been named for her.

SEVEN

The House of Nature was already popular, but after the president's visit, it became extremely popular. Everyone wanted to do what the Darnfields were doing. People began their own vegetable gardens in backyards and driveways, on rooftops and balconies. They started tiny gardens on the roofracks of cars, on window ledges, in rusty wagons and thrown-out briefcases, old tin cans and empty milk cartons. (No one had much luck with indoor gardens, though. Nobody knew the Darnfields' secret—not even the Darnfields, as you may remember—except for Gertie and Thomas.) Parents let their children keep worms and beetles and bats and birds in their rooms. In school, children studied nothing but green plants and ecology, whether they were doing math or reading or social studies or science. Everyone carried around seeds and plants and little pets in their pockets. Mrs. Axel got used to snakes in lunchboxes.

Dozens and dozens of tourists had come to the House of Nature before. Now hundreds and hundreds came, and they threatened to turn into thousands and thousands. The Darnfields were kept busier and busier getting things ready for the crowds, and then cleaning up after the crowds had left. Plants got trampled and had to be staked up. Some of the smaller animals got stepped on. Some animals were very shy, and the noise of the people drove them into hiding. Late in the day they had to be coaxed out gently with baskets of peanuts.

One Saturday morning Gertie and Thomas looked out together from the attic windows. The earliest tourists stood far below, chatting with each other and pointing up to this spot or that on the Darnfields' house.

"You know what?" said Gertie. "Sometimes I wish I could change everything back."

"How come?"

"It's not that I want to right now. Only, I'd like to be able to. What if we needed to change back for some reason? How could we do it?"

Thomas picked a weed and chewed on its crisp, sweet stem. "I don't have any idea, unless we found something else magic to undo it. I don't know what that would be. If you find one magic thing in your lifetime, that's usually it. You can't expect to go on finding them."

"I suppose not," said Gertie.

"I've been trying to figure this out, though," Thomas

went on. "The thing is, what happens if the magic wand or wishbone gets turned into something else?"

"Like what? A magic branch? Or a magic chicken?"

"No, I mean, what if Al *did* eat the wishbone? Wouldn't it turn into Al? And wouldn't he be sort of a wishing alligator?"

"Do you think so?"

"Makes sense to me."

"Mmmmmm." Gertie was not entirely sure. "We can try it, that's what. If we need to, we'll get hold of Al and try him."

Melrose's antlers grew as summer approached. Each branching bone grew until he wore a full set of curved antlers as handsome as a crown. The warmer weather made him restless. Gertie had to let him out of their backyard so that he could walk up and down the streets nearby. Everyone knew who he was; and most people didn't mind that he browsed in their yards. Mrs. Watson was quite put out, however, when he nibbled all the little green cherries off her cherry tree. They were just starting to ripen.

From time to time Gertie and Thomas caught sight of Al. They would make out a pattern of scales among dark leaves; or a pair of small rocks in a pool would bubble, and they would know that the "rocks" were Al's nostrils. Then, when they looked closely, they could see the outline of his head beneath the surface. They couldn't coax him out of the water, though.

EIGHT

Spring had turned to summer. As the sun got stronger and the warm days longer, all the growing things inside the house grew even more. Some plants were familiar; some were strange; some were familiar, but growing strangely. Gertie woke one morning with her sleeping bag tipped up at an angle by a kudzu vine. The vine had not been there yesterday. Now a single strand was elbowing its way beneath the corner of her sleeping bag and down the front hall and out the door. Bunches of shiny green leaves unfolded from its woody stem, and by afternoon reddish purple flowers appeared at the tip.

Other vines and huge, flowering bushes sprang up and spread. They draped themselves over logs and shinnied up the banisters. Colors glowed everywhere, even in the dark. Gertie found purple and red daisies as small as her fingernail. A bush of giant, luminous yellow roses shone all night outside Melrose's shed. Blossoms shaped like stars, horns, cups and bows, bells and bunches of ribbons, opened in the darkest corners. The vines grew so thick that they obscured the walls and seemed to have actually turned into walls. In some places patches of jungle appeared, in others patches of wilderness. Wildflowers and weeds crowded into the closets.

The thick new growth blocked out all the noises from cars, dogs, trucks, motorcycles. Inside the house, one seemed to be farther from the street than was logical. Gertie thought it made everything more interesting. There were shady, uncertain places into which she could walk much deeper than she would have expected. Sometimes, when she and Thomas stood in the shadows or beside bushes, no one could see them. They hadn't become invisible, exactly; but they blended in completely.

Some of the people who came to the Darnfields' house said that something "strange" happened to them there. They felt they had been there much longer than their watches recorded. They seemed to have been very far away. It was hard to pinpoint the moment when the feeling came over them. Was it when they rounded the first bend, after the music room, and smelled a strange perfume from a bank of flowering bushes? There was nothing much to it—simply a pleasant, wandering sensation. Some people liked this, but other people did not.

A few tourists complained.

Then, whatever it was that was happening inside the house began to spread. One morning the band shell in

the city park suddenly was wildly decorated with orange
trumpet vines. Moss that had lingered for years in the
cracks in the brick paving spread afresh across the bricks
and glowed vividly green.

The mayor of the city found that a honeysuckle branch
had forced its way beneath the window of his sixth-floor
office and was extending new, creamy blossoms across his
file cabinet. Bees wiggled in through the window crack
and flew about pollinating with their yellow-dusted
bodies. The sweet smell and peaceful droning made it
hard to concentrate. The mayor, who was an obliging

sort of person, opened the window wider for the bees, put his feet up on his desk, and napped.

The little gardens that people started in their old milk cartons began to be unusually productive. One child found a nest of sweet peas blossoming out of the dirt collected in his jeans pocket seams. There seemed to be many more chipmunks and squirrels than there had been. A family of opossums moved into the gymnasium at the YWCA. A docile mountain lion was seen on the west side of the park.

All the new growth in the House of Nature made more work for the Darnfields.

"Henry, we can't keep up with this much longer. And if we don't keep up with it, everyone will get lost in the swamps," said Mrs. Darnfield one day. She and Mr. Darnfield stood beneath the fronds of a giant fern. At sunrise the fern had been knee-high. By midday it towered over them like a beach umbrella.

"What would be the harm of losing a few tourists?" grumbled Mr. Darnfield. "Natural selection, you know."

"Henry Darnfield! What a thing to say! And with the children listening, too! Still, I know what you mean."

The mowed paths grew back overnight. The Darnfields had to get up and begin chopping away the first thing every morning, in order to keep the paths clear for the visitors. Pushing through thickets of reeds and tall grass was hard work. "This is supposed to be a vacation, not an expedition," one man grumbled. He had just waded through two rooms of cattails as tall as his head. He kept waving his arms to bat away mosquitoes.

In some places the house smelled, especially in hot weather. There were several different smells. The Darnfields liked them all—manure, damp straw, chicken feathers. But the tourists were used to suburban smells—gasoline fumes, MacBurger restaurants, swimming pool chlorine. Some people said the house smelled bad, and they said it was probably a health hazard.

Little by little, the number of tourists shrank, and the number of plants grew.

Finally, one Saturday, a large tomato dropped off its vine onto Mrs. Wood's head. She had been having a hard time that morning. Only two people had wanted to go through the house, and they both kept slipping on boggy places in the path. She had had to stop again and again to help them get back up on their feet. "I do wish your house were better behaved," she said, as she combed the tomato seeds out of her hair. She looked down at her apron pocket, into which a pea vine was extending a curly tendril. "That thing is picking my pocket!" She brushed it away.

"We are trying our best," said Mr. Darnfield. "But this house seems to have a life of its own."

"You're right about that," Mrs. Wood said. "This house does have a life of its own. Have you ever thought of shutting it down for a few days, and trying to get it back into shape? It was so nice before. Maybe if you took out some of the plants, or drove away some of the animals?"

"Now *that* makes sense," said Mrs. Darnfield, secretly pleased. She longed to be rid of the tourists.

"We'll close it today," said Mr. Darnfield.

He painted a wide strip of wood with the words CLOSED FOR REPAIRS and nailed the strip across the sign in front of their house.

The next morning, the Darnfields did a bit of mowing and clipping. They cut back branches here, and chopped out moss there. They scooped up some of the trout and took them to the pond in the city park. They captured a few chipmunks and raccoons and set them free in the country.

It was pleasant work, and they liked the results. Each room looked trimmer and tidier and beautifully green, as if rain had just fallen.

They had lunch.

After lunch, Mrs. Wood stopped by. She had been thinking the entire situation over, and now she had a new and better idea. What if the Darnfields cleaned everything out of the house until next year? "You could hire a cleaning service," she said. "Professional cleaners could make short work of this. And you could call the Animal Rescue League to come and take away the animals. No, wait! I know! You could sell the animals to a zoo!"

Gertie pictured Melrose with a plastic thread around his neck and a price tag: $9.99.

"But why should we do all that?" asked Mrs. Darnfield.

"Well—it's hard to know how to tell you this. But— lots of people have been complaining about the plants. They are popping up everywhere, not just where you plan for them to be. And on hot days, the House of Nature smells. Anyway, nowadays most people are going to the White House Nature Room instead. If you aren't making money from your house, why do you want to keep it like this?"

"One reason is that we like living this way," said Mrs. Darnfield. "We're used to it. I can't imagine what it would feel like to sleep in a bed or buy a box of frozen peas."

"But surely you don't mean to live this way all year round."

"Even longer. We will live this way for as long as it suits us," said Mr. Darnfield firmly.

"Oh, dear! You can't do that."

"Why not?" asked Mrs. Darnfield.

"It's hard to say exactly." Mrs. Wood's face turned red, and she began to snap and unsnap her purse in her embarrassment. "It's just that people do have their expectations of their neighbors." There was an awkward silence. "Enough is enough!" Mrs. Wood went on. "All good things must come to an end."

No one saw exactly what happened next. Mr. and Mrs. Darnfield saw a blur and heard a shriek. Mrs. Wood saw a scaly paw beside her ankle. Gertie saw Al dart out from somewhere with amazing speed and scoop up Mrs. Wood's leather pocketbook in his jaws. He gulped it down and ran behind the waterfall.

Everyone was so surprised, they couldn't help screaming. It was the first time Gertie and Thomas had seen Al for weeks.

"What happened to Mrs. Wood?" Gertie's father was asking. He looked around in alarm. She, too, had disappeared.

"I'm up here." Mrs. Wood's tearful voice floated down to them from a high perch in a tree at the end of the hall. "I was nearly killed!"

"Al really isn't dangerous," Gertie pleaded.

But it was clear that Mrs. Wood didn't believe her.

NINE

On Wednesday morning, Gertie was raking the front hall when she heard a cross voice grumbling to itself: "Where's the blasted bell?"

"The door's open," she called out. She put down her rake and pulled apart the curtain of vines. A man was standing there. He wore a dingy gray suit. He jumped back and frowned when he saw her.

"I have orders to tack up this notice here," he said. He held up a garish orange cardboard sign that said CONDEMNED in black capital letters and, below that, PER ORDER OF DEPARTMENT OF PUBLIC HEALTH AND SAFETY. "First I notify the occupants. That's you. Then I tack up the sign." He bent over and hummed a little tune as he rummaged through his large black satchel.

"What does that mean, *condemned*?" asked Gertie.

"Condemned? It means you've had it. Joan of Arc. Mary Queen of Scots. Murderers in jail, condemned to die. Heads chopped off!" He looked as if he were trying hard not to smile. Gertie saw that he enjoyed frightening her. "When you have a house that's condemned, that means it isn't fit for human habitation. Full of pests or rats, or termites. Once I saw a house condemned because it was full of cats. Eighty or ninety cats."

"We have only two," Gertie said.

"And what about that beast in the back, the wild beast?"

Gertie could hear Melrose snoring behind the house.

"And not to mention the monster," the man went on. "We heard all about your man-eating monster."

"Al has never eaten any people, not even one bite!"

"Look here. My job isn't explaining, it's just putting up the sign." The man pulled a staple gun from the satchel. Gertie could see other orange CONDEMNED signs packed neatly inside.

"Once a house is condemned, that means you've got to move out." The man forgot that explaining wasn't his job, and he went on explaining. "Once a house is condemned, we move in and tear it down." He pointed with the staple gun toward the end of the street. A large, yellow bulldozer spattered with mud was parked there. "Pretty soon we'll bring the rest of our wrecking equipment around, and the day after tomorrow, we'll be ready to roll at dawn." The man looked regretful, but full of his duty.

"Wrecking equipment? But this is our house," said Gertie.

"Yes. Well—I don't make the decisions, little lady. I just tack up the signs."

"I see," said Gertie. But she didn't see at all. And she hated being called "little lady." "There's nothing here that would hurt anyone. Look at how healthy we are. I haven't had a cold in months."

"I couldn't say nothing about that," said the man. He shot staples into the four corners of the sign, fastening it to the house. Gertie flinched at each loud snap of the gun. A passing caterpillar was stabbed to one cardboard corner.

"Now, is your mother here? I need to read this paper to her. It's an Emergency Declaration."

Gertie ran to find her mother. Mrs. Darnfield was in the music room, cutting ornamental grasses. She was going to hang them in bundles to dry in the attic, where they would turn a golden yellow and the seeds and leaves would form beautiful shapes.

"Mom!" Gertie cried. "There's a strange man who's just tacked a sign on our house and he says it's condemned. You have to come while he reads something."

"He's doing what?"

"Come and see. It's awful!"

Mrs. Darnfield gasped when she saw the sign. "I've

never heard of a house being condemned because it was full of plants," she said.

"Is that right," the man said. "Now, I have to read this to you." He read from his piece of paper in a mechanical voice: "We, the citizens of this city, declare that this house at 14 Carneby Road is a health hazard and has put this city into a state of emergency, and we demand that you get rid of all the plants, and take your animals to a zoo or turn them loose in the woods, except for the alligator, which must be turned over to our town warden. . . ." He went on for some minutes. He had turned red by the time he finished reading. He did not look either Gertie or Mrs. Darnfield in the eye, but swept his gaze up the lush, thick-leaved staircase. "It's disgraceful," he said. "We'll give you two days to clear out."

"Two days!" Mrs. Darnfield's voice rose in horror. "If this is all because of that silly reptile . . . ." Her words trailed away. "We must call your father immediately."

The man turned on his heel, picked up his satchel, and hopped heavily down the steps.

Mr. Darnfield started for home at once. He saw the ugly sign the moment he drove around the corner.

"Now, what exactly did this fellow say?" Mr. Darnfield asked, when he had come in and gathered everyone to-

gether. By now Gertie could no longer remember anything he had said *exactly* except the word "condemned."
"He said in two days they're going to tear down our
house," she said. She felt like crying, but she thought
it would be better if she didn't. She heard her voice get
awfully high and tight sounding. "And I know it's all
my fault!"

"All your fault?" Mr. Darnfield was sitting beside
Gertie with his arm around her shoulders. "What makes
you say that? You're not the one who's causing all the
trouble."

"But I mean . . . I was the one who wished for all the
plants, and then the alligator came, and all."

"You wished for them?"

"With the wishbone. And look what happened."

"The wishbone? What wishbone?"

"I found a wishbone, and Thomas made me break it,
and I made a wish, and it came true."

Mr. Darnfield laughed. "A wishbone! Oh, Gertie, what
a worrywart you are! This house is all of our doing. Wishbones are just an old wives' tale," Mr. Darnfield reassured her. "We have all worked together to make our
house full of green growing things." He wasn't quite
right, Gertie knew that, but she felt reassured, none-
theless.

"I can't even remember what our life used to be like,"

Mrs. Darnfield joined in. "In fact, I can scarcely remember how it all got started. Isn't that funny?"

Gertie swallowed hard and looked at Thomas.

"It was when you made me throw away the vacuum cleaner," said Mr. Darnfield. "Remember that? Then afterward, things just grew on their own."

"Oh right, right! Now I remember! What a wonderful feeling that was. Gertie said something to me, I can't recall what, and all of a sudden I felt light and carefree, and out went the vacuum cleaner, just like that." Mrs. Darnfield laughed, remembering again the light, slightly dizzy feeling that had come over her. It was how she had always imagined flying would feel.

"That was when I made the wish with the wishbone," said Gertie.

Her father gently shook his head. "You have an overactive imagination, along with that green thumb of yours," he said. "Still, it is puzzling that people change their minds about whether they like something. Some people get bored, and always want something new. Other people can't stand change. They always want things to stay the same—tidy and predictable. But it really is a nuisance, I suppose, to have our plants turning up all over town."

"Will they really tear down our house?" asked Gertie, who still felt the weight of her private responsibility.

"We don't want to take that chance," her father said. "They could do that. They have torn down condemned houses in the past. Here's what we'll do. Your mother and I will go over to the Department of Health right now and ask for an extension of time and an exception to the rule."

Mr. and Mrs. Darnfield took their best clothes out of the closet, brushed out the spiders and daddy-longlegs, and left for the Health Department's main office.

Gertie and Thomas watched them drive off. They looked almost normal, except that a large geranium was growing in Mr. Darnfield's buttonhole, and Mrs. Darnfield's dress was decorated with a mantle of pea vines.

"Oh, dear!" Gertie wailed. "They don't realize how they look! They don't even know how the house got this way. I told them. Why didn't they believe me? Thomas, what are we going to do? We're the only ones who know what happened."

"Well, I told you I didn't know much about wishbones," said Thomas. Fright made him momentarily cross.

"Do you still think it takes magic to fix magic?"

"Of course it does. You can't mix magic and nonmagic. Who ever heard of that?"

"If only we could find Al and try him out," Gertie said.

"That's what I keep thinking. But he was too quick

the other day. And we don't even know for sure that he's a wishing alligator."

"Well, but we have to do something. What are we going to do?"

"I just don't know!"

"You don't have to get mad about it."

"Gertie, sometimes you're dumb."

"And you're a pain in the neck."

Thomas stomped upstairs to repair a bridge. Gertie wandered around to Melrose's window and gave him a pat on the nose. His antlers had almost outgrown his double window. They would have to widen the window some more—if they still had a house for a window to be in.

Gertie drifted to the chicken coop in the backyard and peered into the darkness. The warm, dusty smell was comforting. As her eyes got used to the dark, Gertie could make out rows of chickens roosting next to one another, feathery mounds with their narrow yellow claws tucked nearly out of sight. She counted the chickens. Thirty. An idea went *click* in her head. If she was looking at thirty chickens, she was looking at thirty wishbones. One of them could be another magic wishbone. It was possible.

"Thomas! Thomas! The chickens!" she called, racing back into the house.

"What's the matter with them?"

"One of them might have a magic wishbone!"

Thomas leaped down the mossy staircase. "Gertie, you're not half as dumb as I thought."

The two children stood on the bottom rail of the half-door that closed the chickens in their coop. A fat brown hen ran back and forth, clucking softly and picking up kernels of corn. Her red comb wobbled as she looked up at the children. She clucked once, as if to scold them.

"But how do we get *to* the wishbone?" Gertie asked.

Thomas made a grim slicing gesture with his finger across his throat. They both looked solemnly at the brown hen, who went about her business pecking at the grain on the floor of the coop.

Gertie tried to make herself feel mean. "Don't you think we better catch one?" she asked.

"Then what?"

"Well, maybe we could take it to the grocery store and the man at the meat counter would kill it for us. And then he could chop it up and get the wishbone."

"I don't know if they do that."

"We'll just have to tell him how important it is."

"Okay. Let's get one."

"Let's get that one." Gertie pointed to a hen. The hen was standing still, so Gertie could see circular patterns of black edges on her white wing feathers. The children climbed over the gate. The chickens ran from them, spreading out across the dirt yard and squawking. Gertie and Thomas circled around the white hen. She ran faster, making indignant noises. They came closer, trapping her in a corner. She darted through their legs. Finally Thomas dived for her and scooped her up in his arms. A few pinfeathers swirled around his shoulders. The hen looked jerkily from side to side and tried to ruffle her wings. Her feet tried to run, twitching against the front of Thomas's shirt. Her red comb trembled. The beautiful pattern on her wings went askew as she tried again and again to stretch her body and escape. Gertie thought about how the hen must feel. The hen pecked at Thomas's arm.

"What do you think the chances are that it's really got a magic wishbone?" she asked in a discouraged voice.

"Not too good," said Thomas.

"Let's think of something else."

The hen got away as Thomas loosed his grip.

"I don't think the grocery store man would even know how to kill it," Gertie went on. The hen lost herself in the crowd of pecking chickens. "I wish Al would come out. I wish the house looked so much like a forest that they couldn't even find us. I wish I had a fairy godmother."

But her wishing did no good.

Mr. and Mrs. Darnfield were gone for three hours. They returned looking glum. "It's no use," Mrs. Darnfield told the children. "We have to follow their orders. All they did was say 'This is our standard procedure, this is our standard procedure.'" Mrs. Darnfield shook her head. "Of course," she went on, "if we do clean up everything, then they can't tear down the house. So at least we can think of that. The house won't be a health hazard any more. It will just be a house. We'll rip everything up and toss it into garbage bags. We can drain the salt pond and the trout streams into the gutter. Garbage trucks will carry away all our vines and fruit trees and moss and white sand and leave them at the city dump. We'll shoo the animals out, and the ones that won't go will have to be captured with nets and taken away. They'll probably have to knock Melrose out with a tranquillizer and carry him off to a zoo. And I don't even want to talk about what lies ahead for the alligator. Then we will buy furniture again. Eat at a table, sit on a sofa, use a vacuum cleaner."

"That sounds terrible!" cried Gertie.

They worked steadily all afternoon. By supper time they had ripped everything out of the kitchen. The backyard was littered with chunks of turf, and a number of apple trees lay outdoors, roots and branches sticking up any old way. Sticks, stones, mud, grass, and torn vines were strewn all over the ground. The kitchen was nothing but bare walls and bare floors. The cats hissed angrily beneath the wood stove. The Darnfields were exhausted, and the sight of the kitchen made them sad. Every shelf and cupboard was clean and empty. It couldn't fail to please the Department of Health.

"Well, I'm hungry," Mrs. Darnfield announced, trying to sound cheerful. "What shall we have for supper?"

"Chicken!" said Gertie and Thomas at exactly the same moment.

"How nicely you children are getting along," Mrs. Darnfield observed.

There was no time for cooking. Mr. Darnfield went out to get boxes of Factory Fried Chicken, even though that went against all the Darnfields' principles. Mrs. Darnfield set out the bulging, greasy boxes on the dinner blanket. Gertie crunched through her crisp chicken pieces. Actually, she loved Factory Fried Chicken. She inspected all the chicken bones closely, and she saw Thomas doing the same thing. But the wishbones had long since been cut apart. Everyone knows that you have to break a wishbone yourself to activate its powers.

After supper, Gertie carried the boxes and paper napkins and straws to the trash cans in the backyard. When she came back in, she noticed that the kitchen looked softer in the twilight, no longer so cold and bare. She looked closer. Very small green shoots with very small green leaves were poking through the cracks between the tiles. In the corners and on the walls and along the edges of the ceiling grew the faint beginnings of new plants.

"Hey! Stuff is growing back!" Gertie called to the others. "Come look!"

Within an hour, as twilight darkened into night, the vines and strawberries and berry bushes made a visible reappearance, and they continued to grow.

"Don't you see?" Mr. Darnfield said, chuckling. "This proves it."

"Proves what?" asked Mrs. Darnfield.

"We can't clean out the house," said Mr. Darnfield. "It simply restores itself. The plants look stronger the second time around. We just gave the kitchen a good pruning, that's all."

"Mmm-hmm." Mrs. Darnfield's face was an odd mixture of worry and relief.

"Now what?" asked Mr. Darnfield.

No one had an answer.

TEN

$\mathcal{B}$y morning the kitchen had grown back. There were new grapes on the vines, bursting with juice. The blueberry bushes were full of huge, silvery blue fruit. Bright red cherry tomatoes dotted the low tomato plants, and three rows of new corn had sprung up by the cellar door.

The Darnfields ate a quiet breakfast. Nobody even mentioned the CONDEMNED sign until the last crumb of cornbread had been carried away by three ants. Then they all began to worry at once.

"Will they come with the bulldozers, like the man said?" Gertie asked.

"I'm afraid the answer is yes," her mother replied.

"If we stand right in front of the house, they'll have to stop," Thomas said.

"They would just arrest us," Mrs. Darnfield said.

"What about the animals?" Gertie asked. "They'll get hurt if they're in the house when the walls fall down!"

"We'll do our best," her father said. This time he did not sound reassuring.

The telephone rang constantly. Some people who called told the Darnfields that they were getting what they deserved, and it was high time, too. Others, who were their friends, called to offer a place to sleep. Some people made suggestions.

"Herbicide!" Mrs. Darnfield hung up the telephone. "Can you imagine? Margaret Harris just called to tell me to use herbicide! That would be murder!"

"What's herbicide?" asked Gertie.

"Plant poison," her mother replied.

In the afternoon a yellow bulldozer drove up and parked at the foot of the hill near the other one. Then a yellow machine with a long neck and a wrecking ball lumbered up on treads and parked beside the bulldozers. Then two enormous dump trucks pulled up next to the wrecking machine.

Just before five o'clock, Gertie slipped out of the house and walked all the way to Mr. Penny's hardware store, pulling an empty red wagon behind her. A sign on the front door said that the store closed at five. Through the glass, Gertie could see Mr. Penny still inside. She knocked on the glass and opened the door. Mr. Penny turned around when he heard the bell that hung on the back of the door.

"Hello, Mr. Penny," she said shyly.

"Hello there, Gertruda." Mr. Penny's voice was slow. He always took his time with everything, including conversation.

"Can I come in?"

Mr. Penny considered this in silence. She looked so worried and so serious that he could not say no. "I'm just straightening up," he said, beckoning her in and closing the door behind her. Mr. Penny's store smelled of keys. By the front counter he kept his key-cutting machine, and behind it hung rows and rows of brass keys. The smell of the metal filings lingered in the air. In his store, Mr. Penny had stacks of things, all in perfect order. He knew where anything was that anyone might want. Spools of chain sat on the floor, and on the shelves were jelly glasses in boxes of six, wallpaper, clocks, clothespins, plastic bags, sandpaper, mops, wrenches; thermometers, ladders, paint chips in graduated colors, electric light switches, Halloween masks. At the moment, Mr. Penny was sorting nails.

"What can I do for you?" he asked, going back to his task.

Gertie explained what she wanted, and what she

wanted it for. Mr. Penny kept sorting nails. After he had put the last nail into the last bin, he said, "I have what you want. I keep it in the back, because it is so powerful, and I only sell it to my special customers. Bring your wagon with you." Gertie followed him down the aisle of garden tools, through the small room where Mr. Penny did his accounts, and into the back of his store. He pulled down five heavy brown bags from a high shelf and stacked them in her wagon. "Follow the directions, just what's written here on the front. It's very simple."

Gertie felt in her jeans pocket for her change purse.

"Let me put it on your family's account," Mr. Penny offered. "We'll settle later. Right now, you have work to do. I'm sorry to hear about all this trouble. I am very fond of that house of yours." He gave her a warm smile.

"Thanks, Mr. Penny," said Gertie.

She pulled the heavy wagon all the way home and parked it just inside the front gate.

Scarcely anyone could touch a bite of supper, though the house had produced its most luscious last crop for them. Each tender, rosy raspberry made Mrs. Darnfield want to weep. They spread their sleeping bags for the last time on the thick grass of the floor. Perfume from the bank of honeysuckle drifted across their faces, and soon, despite their burden of worry, the Darnfield parents fell asleep.

When she was sure her parents were sleeping, Gertie poked Thomas and sat up, rustling as little as possible. Thomas eased himself out of his sleeping bag and stole after her through the house, out the back door, and around Melrose's lean-to.

"What are we doing?" Thomas whispered.

"I'll show you."

They half-tumbled, half-slid down the hill. Under the purple streetlight the five yellow machines sat, tall and misshapen. Their hoods and chrome grilles smiled. Chunks of earth sprouting helpless weeds were caught in the treads of the wrecker's wheels, wheels that towered six feet above them. Gertie and Thomas giggled wildly, and their giggles rang strange echoes from the metal fenders. Right beside one of the bulldozers, Gertie noticed a strand of the kudzu vine, starting to twine up around the main axle.

"You see that?" She pointed to the growing tip of the vine.

"Yeah, well, what about it?" said Thomas.

"We've got to get lots and lots of water."

"What good will water do?" Thomas hurried after her up the hill.

"We're not using it plain. We're going to mix it with this stuff I got from Mr. Penny."

They filled six pails and three watering cans from the

backyard hose and carried them down to the wagon. Gertie tore open the top of one of the brown bags. It was too dark for Thomas to read the label.

"What is it, Gertie?"

"You'll see. Hurry."

The children mixed buckets of water and Mr. Penny's special powder. They crawled around beneath the wheels of the crane and the bulldozers, soaking the ground with the mixture.

As soon as they had emptied all the pails and cans, they raced up the hill to refill them and mix a second batch. As they made their third trip, they could see tiny green leaves unfolding from the tips of the kudzu vine. By the tenth trip, the vine had made several turns around the axle and was feeling its way toward the engine. They began watering the plants all around the house with the liquid.

The next morning the sun rose on one of those clear, cool, beautiful days that seem a special blessing to every living thing. Gertie woke with scared knots in her stomach. It will be all right, it will be all right, she told herself. But she didn't believe it, and neither did her stomach. She slipped to a front window and looked down to the foot of the hill. At least that had worked. All five machines appeared to have been changed overnight into giant hedges shaped like two bulldozers, a crane, and two trucks. From every surface, huge green leaves like elephants' ears waved in the wind. The machines couldn't possibly be driven. Not yet. The Magi-Gro had done its job. "Your garden transformed," the label said. "Use sparingly."

But that wasn't all. Once the vine had enveloped the yellow machines, it had gone on growing. It had continued up and down their street, wrapping itself around everything—cars, fences, doghouses, neighbors' houses. The Darnfields could hear faint cries of distress from all directions as townspeople opened their second-story windows to call for help.

"They'll never get us now!" Thomas crowed.

A little crowd of the people who were able to leave their houses had gathered in front of the Darnfields' gate. Some of them were marveling at the plant sculptures. A few, with pinched, ugly grins, were saying they could hardly wait to see that nature-infested house come tumbling down. Gertie caught sight of Mr. Penny, smiling to himself as he looked at the greenery. She waved to him, and he gave her a salute.

A group of three men wearing overalls approached the bulldozer, hacking a path with axes. Behind them came men carrying chain saws.

"They can't cut through this!" Thomas said. Green

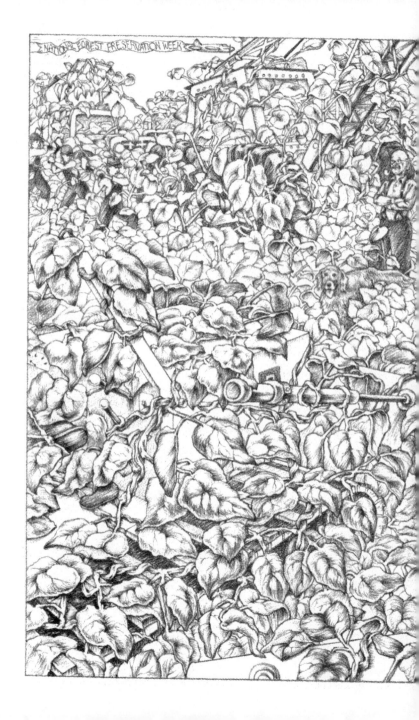

tendrils wrapped themselves around the men's legs as they swung their axes.

Little by little, though, the men did chop and cut a path through the leaves and vines. The first workman reached the bulldozer at noon. He climbed into the driver's seat and started the engine. It gave several backfires and sent out a cloud of evil-looking blue smoke. At twelve-thirty, a second man reached the cab of the crane, climbed into it, and started its engine. A high, whining noise was followed by a buzzing and grinding of gears and then the roar of the motor. The man tried out the gears and levers, raising the heavy wrecking ball up and down. Its chain creaked, and it swung from side to side.

From her window, Gertie watched the machines approach, inch by inch. They would lurch forward a few feet, and their treads and wheels would flatten everything they crossed. As soon as they stopped, new vines wrapped themselves around the wheels and tugged at the ankles of the drivers. But the machines were making progress. It was only a matter of time until they would be at the door.

Animals were scurrying everywhere underfoot, and birds were swooping frantically near the ceiling. They were being crowded out of their burrows and nests by the swiftly growing plants.

"This, I'm afraid, is it," Mr. Darnfield said to Mrs. Darnfield. They prepared to leave. Mrs. Darnfield collected her black frying pan, the picnic blankets, and her basket of garden tools. Mr. Darnfield made a pile of his sweaters and work gloves and hammers. But when they tried to take their things out the front door, Mr. and Mrs. Darnfield made an alarming discovery. They could not get out. The first floor of the house was wound in vines as tightly as a ball of yarn, and the Darnfield family was trapped within.

"Now how are we going to get out?" Mr. Darnfield said. "It's bad enough that they want to tear down our house. But I'm darned if they are going to take me with it!"

"We'll have to climb out a second-story window, or go up to the roof," said Mrs. Darnfield. "Where are the children? Gertie! Thomas! Thomas! Gertie!"

Gertie was upstairs in her closet, gathering her things together. She took down her parka from the pear tree branch, as well as two pairs of sneakers hanging by their laces, and she tried to tuck a lumpy bundle of red velvet dress and puzzles beneath her other arm. The dress and puzzles slipped out. She dropped everything and put on her parka and draped the sneakers around her neck by their laces. Then she picked up the dress and puzzles and looked around for anything else she could take with her. She was in a hurry to leave, for the grass on the floor of the closet was getting taller. It was as high as her waist.

When she heard her mother calling, Gertie came out of the closet. That was when she saw Al. He was comfortably sunk in the mud, in his old spot in Gertie's pond.

"Well, where have you been?" she exclaimed. There was scarcely any water in the pond. It was almost choked with reeds. Like the other animals, Al must have been crowded out of his secret corner (wherever it was) by the growing plants, and he had come back to Gertie's room, looking for a familiar resting spot.

Gertie squished into the mud. Al deftly backed away.

"Hey, hold still, you!" Gertie said. "How can I try you out? If you're a wishing alligator, stand still."

Al slid back three more feet. Gertie dropped her bundles and stretched out flat on the grass beside the muddy pond. She thought she would wriggle closer and reach out with one hand to touch Al. As she lay down, something in her parka poked her in the stomach. She sat up. With trembling hands, she snatched off the parka and felt through the cloth. Something was caught in the lining. She worked it up through the hole in the pocket, and there they were again, the two pieces of the wishbone. They must have been there all along.

"Thomas!" Gertie yelled, at the same time as her

mother was calling below. "Thomas! Where are you? Come in here, quick!"

Her brother thumped down from the attic. He had been leaning out a window trying to throw an escape rope to a nearby oak tree. "Look what I found!" Gertie said.

"You got it back! Where was it?"

"In my parka! It must have been there all along."

"Oh, Gertie, hurry. You've got to use it fast!"

Gertie opened her mouth to make a wish. But which one? So many possibilities tumbled through her mind at once. She could wish for the wrecking machines to disappear. But the city could always send more. She could wish for everyone to love the plants instantly, but that wouldn't stop the bulldozers now. She could wish that everything would come out all right in the end, but she hated to leave the particulars to chance. She could try to undo it. But what would the right words be? The noise of the bulldozers and the chain saws came louder and closer.

"I wish everything would go back to the way it was in the beginning!" Gertie cried.

Immediately, there came a shaking and thundering, such a cataclysmic sound of nature going into reverse as has never been heard in the history of the world. Gertie and Thomas were rattled and rolled about as grass retreated into roots, tulips into bulbs, leaves into branches, and branches into trunks; trunks shrank and sank, vines retreated to seeds, whipping around the room so fast in their passage to nonexistence that they sent breezes blowing and scratched Gertie on the legs. By the time she looked behind her, Al was gone. He had left a silhouette pressed into the mud, and in the center of it was a large pale egg. The egg grew smaller, then became transparent, then vanished.

When the grass had almost entirely slipped away from beneath her feet and Gertie could step over the shrinking hedges, she ran downstairs. Thomas came close behind her. Their mother and father were standing in the center of the hallway, clutching their rakes and pans and dodging flying vines and an occasional cucumber that thudded to the floor. Through the front windows—which were rapidly clearing—they could see one of the bulldozers tilted onto its side, and several spectators hopping and leaping to keep their feet from getting tangled in the retreating kudzu vine.

At last, everything was still. Fine dust, and almost nothing else, lay everywhere. One empty bird's nest dangled by a twig from a corner of the library ceiling, and a couple of crushed tulips lay beneath the stairwell. All the birds were gone, and the plants and trees and fish and ponds and animals. The wishing end of the wishbone had vanished with them.

ELEVEN

People talked for days about the "earthquake" that had shaken the Darnfields' hill and ruined the plants and driven away the animals. The timing of the "earthquake" had been such a coincidence, they said. Just when the bulldozers were closing in on the house, the bushes and vines and even whole trees had been uprooted. The house had trembled and rattled. All the pieces of wrecking equipment had been flipped on their sides like Tonka toys. Everyone agreed it was a miracle that the house was still standing. And now, nearly everyone said it was a shame that all the greenery was gone. They missed looking every day to see what new thing was growing out of the House of Nature. They missed the surprise vines twining along the supermarket shelves. The YWCA wasn't the same without the opossum family.

Of course, the Darnfields felt terrible. But they were glad their house was still standing. The same afternoon that the house had been undone, Mrs. Wood came to see if they were all right. Her high heels echoed on the wooden floor. The walls were empty. The rooms looked small and dingy. "It was so wonderful before!" Mrs. Wood said. Tears filled her eyes. "I didn't realize how much I would miss it. Well, dears, your friends will help you out."

They did, starting that very day. People lent them furniture. Mrs. Peapacker had her husband bring over their old pink silk sofa. It felt so peculiar to sit on it. Gertie kept slipping off. Mrs. Walters gave them the contents of her attic—two lumpy chairs and a kitchen table with metal legs. The Williams family lent them some cots to set up in their bedrooms.

Mrs. Wood brought over her old vacuum cleaner. Mrs. Darnfield used it to clean up all the gritty corners of the house. It felt odd, she said to Mr. Darnfield. "It's been so long since I've done this that I can't seem to get the hang of it." Even worse, she had to go grocery shopping right afterward. "I'm not sure I can find my way around a supermarket anymore!" she said.

Soon the pantry shelves and the refrigerator were full of plastic dishes and packages of food. They pulled the two lumpy chairs and two rickety wooden chairs up to the borrowed kitchen table and choked down their dinner. The food looked strange, sitting on plates way up high on the table. The vegetables weren't the right color, and nothing tasted as good as the fruit from their own orchards.

Gertie's cot was too narrow. That first night, she tossed and turned for hours. Her room seemed empty, with only herself in it. There were no night noises to keep her company: no pairs of green eyes glowing briefly at midnight, no owls hooting, no rustling of toads among the leaves, no Melrose bumping in his shed. It was so quiet she thought she would never go to sleep.

In the morning, everyone had a backache. "I can't stand it!" Mr. Darnfield said. That evening he came home from work with a long cylinder, a big, pipe-looking thing, tied to the roof of the car. The thing was wrapped in brown paper. It took all four of them to carry it into the house. Then Mr. Darnfield tore away the brown paper and unrolled a thick green rug. They got their sleeping bags back out, and from then on they slept on the floor on the rug. It wasn't the same, but it was better than sleeping on cots.

News of the house soon reached the president. He wrote a letter to the Darnfields, saying how sorry he was. The Darnfields' house was the only one like it in the entire world. Even the Whittemore Room in the White House wasn't the same as the House of Nature. They were having maintenance problems. Things kept dying off or sprouting out too far, and animals were forever escaping. They were thinking they might have to close it down, and how could they, if the House of Nature didn't exist any more? Where would people go?

"You see, people need our house," Gertie said. "If only they hadn't condemned it."

"Well, it would have gotten all ruined in the earthquake anyway," Mrs. Darnfield reminded her.

"That wasn't an earthquake," Gertie said.

"How's that?"

"Oh, nothing. I was just mumbling."

Summer was gone, school began, and as winter approached, Mrs. Darnfield began to talk reluctantly about buying new furniture. There was always a good excuse not to. "Yes, yes," Mr. Darnfield would say. "Next spring, we'll take this house in hand. We'll put it back to rights. We'll fill in the empty ponds, and take out the pipes, and close up the skylights. But let's wait till spring to do it. Winter isn't a good time for building projects."

The truth was, none of them wanted to change the house back.

They bought sacks of birdseed and fed the birds outdoors. It was strange to have the chickadees landing on a bird feeder. It was strange to look out at clusters of sparrows, all of whom fled into the air like blown leaves if a human being came close to the window. Gertie noticed one sparrow in particular that hopped again and again onto their kitchen window ledge. It always preferred breadcrumbs to birdseed. The way the sparrow hopped and steadily picked up breadcrumbs was so familiar.

Gertie watered her seedlings faithfully. She had found her old rows of paper cups again after the vines disappeared from her room. The lemon and pumpkin sprouts were still in the cups. There was so little sun in January that the seedlings scarcely grew. She captured a few beetles in Allison's basement and brought them home with her. In February two spiders wove webs in the corners of her ceiling. Dirt collected again on her floor and shelves, and then in other rooms in the house. Her mother never did get back into the habit of continuous vacuuming, and nobody said a word about housekeeping.

One morning in March, Gertie saw a ring of little green sprouts in front of her bookshelves. She and Thomas and Allison had been sitting there a few days before, playing Monopoly. Gertie remembered she had eaten an orange during the game and had tossed the seeds over her shoulder.

That was interesting.

A few days later, she happened to look into her dollhouse and saw a thin coat of moss and two tiny flowers growing on the dollhouse floor. She ran for Thomas.

"Just mold," he said skeptically.

"Well, I never heard of mold growing flowers," Gertie said.

The orange seedlings got taller.

The sprouts in the paper cups grew half a foot high.

One wall of the kitchen developed a crack, and something that looked like a grapevine poked a tentative pink leaf through it. Two raccoons turned up on the back porch and appeared to be waiting for something. Mrs. Darnfield set out four apple cores and the tops of some carrots for them. A dozen birds tapped at the windows with their beaks.

The Darnfields didn't dare say a word about any of this at first. They just kept putting out apple cores and scattering birdseed. But when a faint line of grass appeared in a crack in the library floor, Mr. and Mrs. Darnfield decided it was time to take action. If the house was trying so hard to become green again, they would help it. They ordered truckloads of the finest soil. They polished up the skylights and ordered a new batch of trees. They scrubbed out the dry ponds and refilled them.

Mrs. Darnfield returned the borrowed vacuum cleaner to Mrs. Wood.

"I suppose you've bought one of your own now," Mrs. Wood said.

"No, that's not why I'm bringing it back. I have some news for you. I hope you'll be happy to hear this."

"What's that?"

"We're getting the plants back."

"You don't mean it!" Mrs. Wood cried. She gave Mrs. Darnfield a hug of excitement. "Nothing could make me happier! It's just like we said. Your house has a life of its own, and nothing will keep it down, not even an earthquake!"

Mr. Darnfield rolled up the green rug and stored it in the attic. Soon the April sun had brought out buds and grass and berry bushes in the kitchen and the front hall. Mr. Darnfield gave his usual explanation: "Our family has the world's greenest thumbs." He pushed up his sleeves and got out the hoes and rakes and lawn-mower.

By now the newspaper reporters and the television camera crews were back, and soon the news reached the president. He promptly telephoned them. He said how happy he was that they had been able to restore their house. He had just declared it a National Treasure, and from that day on no one would be allowed to knock it down or tell the Darnfields to change one single leaf. There would be no more misunderstandings about condemning it, either. (Though it *would* be best if they confined the plants to the house, and discouraged alligators, and so on, from wandering around freely.) His grandchildren were so excited that he was going to let them come for a visit on their own, just as soon as the Darnfields had everything back in order.

The Darnfields were working night and day to prune and trim and shape and cultivate. Mrs. Wood helped them, and Mr. Penny, and all their friends and neighbors. No one in town complained about the house now. The green leaves in funny places and the trees growing through the skylights were a welcome sight. Gertie's swampy pond reappeared, without any alligator eggs— yet. Mrs. Darnfield ordered a new batch of chickens. The beehives began to hum, and Mr. Darnfield restocked the streams with trout. Mrs. Darnfield planted lettuce in the old library lettuce patch, and soon tiny pairs of first leaves spread in a green haze across the floor.

Everything about the house made Gertie feel good. It was as if an old and favorite friend had returned. Still, glad as she was, she kept wondering why the plants had come back. She thought she had wished them away. She remembered distinctly that she had wished for everything to go back to the way it was in the beginning. She puzzled and puzzled over this.

On the day before the president's grandchildren were coming for their visit, Gertie and Thomas were working in the front hall. They were gathering up bundles of shoots and branches that their father had trimmed from the hedges. Suddenly Gertie dropped her armful.

"Thomas! I've got it! I've just figured it out! Now I see why the plants all came back. When I made that last wish, I really meant to say that I wanted everything to go back to the way it was before any of this happened. But what I said was, I wish everything would go back to the way it was in the beginning. The wishbone thought I meant the beginning of the house turning green. So that's how the whole thing started over again. First the house was bare, with no plants at all. Then dirt piled up. Then the plants started growing at the end of winter, the same as last year."

"I think you've got it, Gertie. Except—if everything is the same as in the beginning, does that mean that everything is going to happen the same, all the way through?"

"No," said Gertie decisively. "What happens after the wish gets started is only up to us."

"Well, that's good."

"But that's not the best part. I just thought of something else."

"What else?" asked Thomas.

"Well, if everything went back to the beginning, then the wishbone must be back where it was at the beginning, too. We haven't looked there for it."

"You really think so?"

"Want to find out?"

They left their heaps of trimmings all over the hall and

put on their sneakers and ran to the park. It was a May morning, full of sunshine and grass and a fresh, sweet wind. A pair of dogs raced playfully beside the children as they crossed the park. Gertie remembered exactly where she had found the wishbone. The trash can was on the far side of the park, near a set of swings.

Gertie scuffed around in the dirt beside the trash can. "It was right on top last year," she said. She pushed some pebbles aside with her foot. "Oh! I knew it! It *is* here!" She picked it up out of the dirt. "Sure looks like the same one." The wishbone was smooth and white, with a perfectly shaped fork.

Thomas took it gingerly in his fingers. "I wonder if I could make the wish this time. I don't think it has to be you."

Gertie knew he was dying to try it. After all, he had been waiting an entire year. "All right. I guess so," she said.

Thomas took a deep breath. "Now. If it is the same one, we've got to be careful what we do with it. We can't make just any old wish."

"Right."

"Like, we could wish for a million more wishbones. But with wishing, if you're greedy, it usually backfires."

"Right. We'd probably get this big pile of bones right here in the park. What a mess. Hmm. We could wish to have everything stay the same for ever and ever. Only . . . that could get boring."

"We could wish to have one wish a year, from now on," said Thomas judiciously.

"We could wish to know how the wishbone works," suggested Gertie.

"I sort of doubt if we'd get that wish."

"Well, don't take a chance on wasting it. Let's think of a nice, good wish that isn't greedy."

"Okay. Here's one. Let's—"

The two dogs had been having a chasing game. One of them, a little brown and white one, was full of playful spirits and wanted to include the children in the game. It came hurtling across the grass. Just as Thomas was saying "let's—" it knocked straight into his legs. Thomas went flying, and so did the wishbone. The dog spotted it where it landed, picked it up in its mouth, and ran off.

Thomas scrambled to his feet. "The dog's got it! Quick! Catch that dog!" He and Gertie chased the dog across the park. The dog, thoroughly enjoying itself, ran ever faster, its ears flapping. When it came to the gate to the park, it darted out. By the time Gertie and Thomas had reached the gate, the dog was out of sight.

"You go that way, I'll go up here," said Thomas, pointing up and down the sidewalk.

They searched for an hour. They asked every person they saw on the street whether a brown and white dog without a collar had come that way. It hadn't. They peeked over porch rails and walked up driveways and looked into backyards, but they didn't see that dog again.

At last they gave up. The search was hopeless. They had to go back. They trailed slowly down the streets toward home.

"That dog is sure going to be surprised if it bites through the wishbone," Gertie said.

"Yeah. Can you just see it? The dog thinks about wanting a bone to eat, and all of a sudden, big bones for it on every corner."

"Yes! It gets cold, and—boing!—a door opens and someone asks it to come in and get warm by the fire."

"Suddenly one day, fields full of rabbits everywhere to chase."

They imagined all the things that the dog's wishing might produce.

Their father was waiting for them. "Where have you been?" he asked. "Tomorrow's a big day. How about finishing up your job here?"

They worked all afternoon. The house looked beautiful at sunset, with everything in readiness for the children's visitors.

The family spread out their sleeping bags.

"You know, Henry, I could do this for the rest of my life," said Mrs. Darnfield.

"Well, dear, that's good, because we are going to. This house needs full-time attention," said Mr. Darnfield.

"Aren't we lucky to have it then, since we like gardening so much?"

A contented snore was Mr. Darnfield's answer.

Gertie wasn't sleepy, and neither was Thomas. "You know," Gertie said in a low voice, "I've been thinking. We didn't really need the wishbone any more. The plants and animals came back, and nobody is allowed to condemn the house ever again, and if we don't pour on any more plant food, we can live here just the way we want to. So we don't need it. The dog needed it worse than we did."

"I know," said Thomas. He still sounded disappointed.

"So don't feel bad, okay?"

"I'll try not to."

A thumping and bumping shook the side of the house. Gertie and Thomas sat up. So did their parents.

"There's only one thing that makes that noise," said Gertie.

"He's back!" shouted Thomas.

All the Darnfields ran to the side porch to open the wide window for Melrose.

MORE BOOKS FROM BEECH TREE

Pete & Lily by Amy Hest. Pete (Patricia) Jaffe and Lily Rosenblume are best friends. Nothing has ever come between the two twelve-year-olds, not even adorable Roger Starr, the class heartthrob. Then Pete's widowed mom and Lily's divorced dad start dating. "Lively and appealing."   —*The Horn Book*
(ISBN 0-688-12490-9; $4.95)

DeDe Takes Charge! by Johanna Hurwitz. It's been a year since DeDe Rawson's parents divorced, but life still hasn't gotten back on track for the fifth grader. If things are to get better, DeDe decides, she'll have to take matters into her own hands. "Fun, fast-paced reading."

—*School Library Journal*
(ISBN 0-688-11499-7; $3.95)

Onion Tears by Diana Kidd. Nam-Huong, A Vietnamese girl, wants to adjust to her new life in Australia, but she can't. She misses her parents and her beloved grandfather too much, and she is haunted by her experiences as a refugee. With the help of her teacher, she begins to love and trust again. ♦ "Profoundly moving."

—*Kirkus* (pointer)
(ISBN 0-688-11862-3; $3.95)